"And now, the m[...]
for. The camp [...]
Bowman!" said M[...]

"For those of you who don't know, it's only fair to warn you," Tom began, in a grave voice. "The name of this place is Camp Slumbering Pines. But to those who know the legend, it will always be...Camp Sasquatch."

I heard a few giggles, but I was starting to feel seriously freaked out. I shivered and hugged my knees to my chest.

"Sasquatch is another name for Big Foot, the creature that roams the woods of the Pacific Northwest," Tom went on. "We tell you guys this story so you'll understand that you can never, never go out alone. You never know when you'll run into a Big Foot. Even now, every once in a while, you can hear one of them howling in the woods."

Tom stopped talking and narrowed his eyes, listening carefully.

No one moved.

Then we all heard it.

A desolate howl, from deep in the woods.

I knew it. The Big Foot were coming, and they were out to get us!

**Read these books in
the SHADOW ZONE series:**

**And zapping your way from
the SHADOW ZONE soon:**

SHADOW ZONE™

SCREAM
AROUND THE CAMPFIRE

BY J. R. BLACK

BULLSEYE BOOKS

Random House ⌂ New York

A BULLSEYE BOOK PUBLISHED BY RANDOM HOUSE, INC.

Library of Congress Catalog Card Number: 94-67607
ISBN: 0-679-87080-6
RL: 4.6

Manufactured in the United States of America   10 9 8 7 6 5 4 3 2 1

1

Welcome to Camp Nowhere

Nature! What a crock.

My parents have come up with some stupid ideas in their time, but this has got to be the absolute stupidest. I mean, okay, I can understand that my mom has to go hang out with my Aunt Sarah for the summer, because Aunt Sarah just had a baby. And I know my dad is busy with his job and all. Television reporting isn't a picnic. But my brother Frank and I are eleven years old! We're not babies anymore.

So why did they have to send us to this dumb summer camp?

I asked them this question about a billion times before they shipped us off to this buggy place. I asked my brother this question five hundred more times while we sat in the Jeep for two hours, riding out of Seattle, into the Cascade Mountains. (He told me to shut up about five hundred times too.) And I asked myself the same question as Frank and I finally stepped out of the Jeep and into Camp Slumbering Pines.

This place was out in the boondocks. Way out. And we were stranded here for a long, boring summer.

Don't get me wrong—summer is the best. There's nothing I like better on a hot day than stretching out on the couch, soaking up the air conditioning, and watching television with a bunch of my friends.

The talk shows are my favorite. All those crazy people talking about how they saw space aliens in their backyard while we take turns making fun of them. And when that gets tired, we can just surf through the channels for whatever's better.

That is, when I can get the remote control away from Frank.

Frank's my twin brother. But he couldn't be less like me. I mean, we kind of look alike. Both of us have green eyes. And both of us are pretty tall. But personality-wise? Like two peas from totally different pods.

First off, and most obvious, he's a boy and I'm a girl. Duh.

Second, he's always running around doing sports. He always tries to make me watch basketball with him. He's a huge Sonics fan, of course. But I never really get into it. Plus, he gets really good grades in school. My parents say I'd do well in school, too, if I'd shut up long enough to hear what the teachers have to say.

Anyway, Frank didn't see why I was so opposed to this camp thing. But I was sure he'd hate it once he saw it.

I sure did.

"What a dump," I breathed to myself as we stood there, surrounded by our duffel bags. There was a big, dank-looking barn on the top of a hill, with pathways going off to either side of it. We were standing on a rundown old field that seemed to be pulling double duty as a baseball diamond and a football field. At the bottom of the hill, there was a lake or river or pond or something. Anyway, it was water, and it wasn't the beach. I couldn't believe I was stuck here for the whole summer!

But here I was, at Camp Dork. Other kids were filing off school buses and running up to greet each other. They screamed and giggled as if they were best friends that hadn't seen each other in a year. Which I guess was true.

That left Frank and me as the outsiders.

No one was running up to us and screaming and hugging, that's for sure. I felt as if Frank and I were invisible. That was fine with me, though.

If these kids didn't want to know me, I didn't want to know them.

I noticed one cluster of girls, about my age, crowding around a teenager with long black hair. She was checking off names on a clipboard.

"Heidi! Heidi," one of the girls yelled.

The mouth belonged to a sturdy girl with a long blond braid. She was hopping up and down like an idiot, trying to get all the attention. What a loudmouth!

Before I knew it, Heidi was walking toward me. I looked over to Frank, but he was already talking to another counselor, a really good-looking guy with shoulder-length blond hair tied back in a ponytail. I was on my own. I took a deep breath and turned around to face Heidi.

"Hey, you must be Gina Giardelli," she said, smiling at me and my dad. People always recognize him from his TV news reports.

"Yeah," was all I could think of to say.

"Well, pick up your stuff," she answered. "We're going to head on up to the cabin."

Pick up my stuff? I barely managed to get my duffel bag out of the house and into the car! I looked at my dad, pleadingly, but he just smiled.

"Have a great summer, kid. And thanks again for agreeing to try this camp."

I hadn't agreed to anything, of course. But

parents seem to have complete power over their kids. Have you ever noticed?

Anyway, Dad waved one last time at me and Frank. Then he drove off...my last hope for escape.

I tried to hoist my huge duffel bag onto my shoulder and fell over twice.

"'Scuse me," someone said behind me.

I turned around. It was one of the girls that had been crowding around Heidi. She was a tiny, wispy thing with mousy hair and huge gray eyes. She definitely didn't look like the Grizzly Adams type.

"Mostly, people help each other with their duffel bags." She pointed at some of the other girls, and I saw what she meant. They had paired off so they each held one end of two bags. It made sense, if you had a buddy to carry the bags with.

"Want me to help you?" the girl asked me, in a whispery voice. "My name is Stacey."

I looked her over again. I mean, her arms and legs looked like toothpicks! But the other girls had already paired off, and Heidi was leading them up one of the paths.

I glanced over my shoulder to look for Frank again. He was already going up the other path with the rest of his bunk. "See you at dinner, Gee," he called.

That left me with Stacey the mouse. I lifted my ends of my bag and Stacey's, and we started slowly up the hill.

The path was endless. I couldn't even tell where it was, at some points. The trees closed in behind us, and it looked as if we were in the middle of the woods. Stacey had a hard time keeping up with the rest of the bunk, no matter how much I tried to drag her along. Finally, she just dropped her end and started shaking her arms.

"Come on," I urged her. The other kids were getting way ahead of us. I didn't know where we were going, and I didn't want to get lost in the woods with Wheezy and two duffel bags.

"Just a second," Stacey said, apologetically. She blew on her hands, which were red and sore. I sat down on my bag, and leaped up again with a shout. Something skittered away from me.

"What was that, a rat?" I shrieked. Then I got a really gross shivery feeling, as if a million ants were running up my spine.

"It was just a raccoon," Stacey said. I think I heard her giggle, but I'm not sure. I was still squinting into the underbrush, standing on one leg. A leaf brushed against me, and I jumped about ten feet in the air. I was totally freaked out.

"Hey!" A loud, angry voice sliced through me. "Get up here. *Now! Move it!*" Stacey jumped and tugged at the bags. I turned and looked. It was Heidi, and she was mad.

"We're tired," I started to say. But she cut me off.

"I can't have you falling behind," she yelled. "I'm the one that gets in trouble if you get separated, and the other girls are way ahead of you. *So get movin'!*"

Nice, I thought. *What is she, a drill sergeant?* I could see how this was shaping up already.

Heidi was just like the high school girls who came to my school to help coach the soccer team. They're sweet as pie one minute, when they feel like they're best friends with us kids. But they totally fly off the handle two seconds later. I guess they're too old to be kids, but they're not quite ready to be grown-ups, either. Anyway, Heidi looked to be in college, which is just a few years older than high school.

"*Now!*" she shrieked.

Grown-up or not, she was in charge of me for the next eight weeks. I jumped, then looked behind me one more time, half-expecting that squirrel-monkey thing to come squealing out of the trees and land in my face. I picked up the bags again.

Finally, after about a billion miles through this total jungle, we got to our cabin.

Did I say cabin?

It was more like a shack! Like on that TV show *M*A*S*H*, with wire for walls and cots inside it. I didn't see a bathroom. Or a shower.

"Home sweet home," the blond-braid girl announced, dragging her bag over the hunk of concrete that served as a stoop and through the front door.

"Linda, can I have the good cot this year?" another girl asked her.

So the bigmouth was Linda.

"We'll flip for it," Linda answered.

"People, I'm heading back down to hand in my checklist," Heidi shouted. "I'll be back in ten minutes, so get settled in." There was a chorus of okays from inside, and Heidi went back down the path.

By the time I lugged my bag inside, the rest of the girls were all halfway unpacked. And they were giggling and whispering about stuff. As I said, they had probably spent about a million summers together in this stupid place, and they were all best friends. They didn't want me there

8

any more than I wanted to be there.

Each cot had a cubbyhole next to it, and there was only one bed left for me—by the door. I couldn't believe how gross this place was. The floors were made of splintery-looking wood.

I can't explain it, but the whole place gave me a really weird feeling in the pit of my stomach. Not a gross-out feeling. More like...something was waiting for me.

Watching me.

And my bed was right there by the door, with nothing but this screen between me and the outside. The hairs on the back of my neck began to stand up....

I shook myself. Sure, this place was dirty, but I was getting pretty carried away! I flopped my duffel bag onto the empty cot and yelped—a humongous, hairy spider was creeping around on the bed. *Yeech.* I whacked at it with one of my flip-flops.

"'Scuse me," Stacey said, behind me. She had the bed next to mine.

"What?" I asked, sharply.

The spider had escaped to a high corner, above the head of my cot. I swear, it was staring at me, trying to decide if I'd taste better baked or fried.

"I always leave them alone," she said in that

whispery, wheezy voice. "They catch the mosquitoes."

I turned around and looked at her as if she were crazy. "Haven't you ever heard of bug spray?"

"Bug spray makes my asthma act up," she said, wrinkling her nose. Then she went back to unpacking her stuff.

I glanced around, and the other girls were kind of looking at me. As if there was something weird about wanting this spider out of my bed.

"Excuse me, is there something wrong?" I said to them, with my best homegirl attitude. My friends at home would have whooped and high-fived me if they had been there to hear.

"Nothing's wrong," said Linda the Mouth, all fake-sweet and nice. "Rebecca, why don't you show her where the showers are."

"Okay," another girl said. She moved to the door. "Come on, they're outside."

Outside? The showers were *outside?* This place was getting grosser by the second.

Rebecca, a tall girl with thick, honey-blond hair, opened a back door and looked at me, her hazel eyes peering through her poodley bangs. She looked nervous about something. I figured my attitude was pretty intimidating—I'm a city girl, after all, and she was some kind of country hick. I followed her out the back door of the cabin.

About ten feet away, there were two wooden shacks. She opened one door, and there was a hole in a piece of wood.

"This is the outhouse," she explained. Then she showed me how to dump lime in the hole. She said it killed the stench. Revolting.

"And this is the shower," she said, opening the door to the other shack.

There was a showerhead in there, all right. A frog hopped out, almost landing on my feet, and I jumped back.

"Nice," I said, repulsed.

"You can put your shampoo and conditioner and soap and stuff in a bucket, and carry it out here in the morning," Rebecca went on, giving a sidelong look at the bunk.

"I guess that's why they told me to bring a bucket," I said.

"Right." Rebecca nodded. I turned to go back into the bunk. I had seen all I wanted to see, out there by the outhouse.

"Wait!" She stopped me. "Um—this is how you turn on the shower." She turned on the spigots. "First hot, then cold. You get only five minutes, so you don't use up all the hot water. It comes from a well."

A well. This was just fascinating.

"That's great," I said, nodding. What did she expect me to do, jump up and down with joy? Why did she want me out here so badly? I turned to go inside again.

"Gina, look!" she said. "This is a salamander." I turned around, exasperated. I was about to tell her that I couldn't care less about her stupid outhouse or her lizards or any of it, but the back door to the cabin opened and Linda stuck her head out.

"Hey, what's taking so long?" she asked.

"Rebecca was just showing me all the great sights," I said sarcastically.

Rebecca grinned and turned away from me. I followed her back to the cabin, wishing for an end to this whole camp thing.

Inside, everybody was quiet, sitting on their bunks. It was weird. I just figured they were trying to freak me out, so I went back to unpacking my bag. I pulled out a pair of shorts. Suddenly I froze. I heard a weird rattling sound. I looked in my bag.

There was a coiled-up snake!

"Look out, Gina!" one of the girls yelled. "Run for your life. It's a rattlesnake!"

2

Rattled!

I screamed and fell backward. The snake slithered out of my duffel bag and into a crack in the floor, where it disappeared from view.

My heart was pounding so hard in my ears, it took a few seconds for me to notice that everybody was laughing!

"What is so funny?" I demanded. "That thing could have killed me!"

Linda just stood there laughing even harder. She took her hand out from behind her back. She was holding a little pink baby rattle.

"It was a garter snake, city girl!" she giggled, giving it a shake. "There are no rattlesnakes in the forest. They live in the desert! Duh, don't you know anything?"

"Oh, that is really funny," I said, standing up and dusting myself off. "You guys are nuts. Is that what you think is funny? Scaring somebody half to death?"

They just kept laughing. My face was burning, and I'm sure it had turned bright pink. I had no idea what to do—I just wanted to run down to the buses and beg someone to take me back to Seattle. I hated these girls!

I stepped over to my cot and just kept unpacking my stuff, refolding my clothes and sticking them into the cubbyhole. Linda and the others came over and stood around me.

"Gina, it was just a joke," Linda said. Her voice was so loud and annoying. She was really getting on my nerves. "You know, like a trick? It happens to all the new kids at the camp!"

"When I was new, they put a frog in my cot," Rebecca said, sitting on my bed. "Don't be mad."

"I'm not mad," I said. "I just think that's really stupid. Don't you people have a life?"

"Well, excuse us," Linda snapped back, and they all just stood there while I kept unpacking. It was silent and uncomfortable. Finally, Heidi came back in and saw us all standing around.

"Chop chop," she said. "Everybody unpacked? Gina, you should be all set up by now."

"They put a snake in my stuff," I said. Then I realized how wimpy that sounded. "They said it was a rattlesnake," I added lamely.

"You guys were doing initiation games? That's totally against the rules," Heidi barked.

The other girls rolled their eyes and went back to their cots while she scolded them.

"Gina's new to this camp, and I want her to feel welcome," Heidi continued, making me feel smaller and smaller. "She doesn't have your experience, and she doesn't understand how much fun camp can be. So no more snakes, and no more jokes, or you'll all be in *big trouble!*"

Oh, boy. Now they really hated me. It was my fault Heidi was yelling, and whatever *big trouble* she had in mind, it probably involved more yelling.

I could see the other girls looking at each other sideways, trying not to laugh while Heidi screamed.

"All right, now everybody get going. It's time for dinner and evening campfire," Heidi announced. Then she slammed out the door to wait for us outside. As soon as she was out of the cabin, Linda and the others started giggling, though they totally avoided my eyes.

"All right, campfire!" Linda said.

Everyone jumped up and started pulling on baseball caps and flannel shirts. They seemed to have forgotten about me again. Apparently, evening campfire was some kind of big deal around here. I sat on my cot and watched them.

"There are some good worms out back," I

heard Linda say to Rebecca. "We'll be able to use them for fishing."

"I can't believe you picked up that snake," Rebecca said to Linda.

"I can't believe you were scared of it," she said back.

Yuck.

Then I noticed that they were all changing their shoes. They were putting on big fat hiking boots, with sweat socks pulled all the way up to their knees. It looked so doofy!

I left on my black Air Jordans, with my purple slouch socks pushed all the way down around my ankles. And why were they all wearing baseball hats? The sun was going down soon, so it wasn't as if they'd need to cover their heads.

As we walked out the door, Stacey fell into step beside me. I noticed she was carrying a little travelsize packet of tissues. She kept dabbing at her nose as she talked to me.

"They did that to me, too, when I first came here," she said.

"Yeah, they do it to everybody." I wasn't interested.

"They put a bug in my sneaker. I got so scared, I started crying."

I looked at her. Crying? What a wimp!

"I was only eight," she added, as if she knew what I was thinking.

I looked down at the ground while we walked and didn't say anything else. I may have been miserable, but I was not about to bond with the camp nerd!

We walked back down the endless pathway to the mess hall, which is what they called that skanky old barn. Inside, the walls were decorated with painted oars and fishing nets.

The campers from each cabin had their own table, and on the boys' side I saw Frank sitting with his bunkmates. He was laughing and joking with the other guys, having a great time. His socks were pulled up to his knees, and he was wearing his Mariners cap. *Traitor!*

He saw me and waved, so I waved back. But it made me really mad. It was bad enough that I hated my own bunk so much. But it was even worse that—as usual—my brother was slipping right in and adjusting perfectly.

How can he have fun in a stupid place like this? I wondered. *What if his friends from home saw him wearing that dorky getup?*

But Frank didn't seem to be thinking about his friends from home right now. He was having a great time.

And I was totally miserable. I chewed on my

cheeseburger and sipped my bug juice, but my stomach was churning. All around me, the girls from my bunk were chattering and laughing and totally ignoring me.

Did you know that you can be surrounded by people and still feel lonely?

3

Howl I Get Out of Here?

By the time we all got settled around the big campfire, it was getting pretty dark.

A bunch of girls were shining their flashlights into each other's eyes so they'd feel as if they were blind. Two girls stuck their flashlights under their chin so they looked like skeletons.

You know, stupid camp stuff like that.

I just kept shining my own flashlight into the grass, to make sure nothing crawled on me. Finally, this big fat guy came out, stood in front of the fire, and introduced himself.

"My name is Henry Creeley, and as of this year I'm in charge of Camp Slumbering Pines!" He spoke in that voice that grown-ups use when they're talking to kids that they think are imbeciles.

"What does he mean, *as of this year?*" I asked Stacey, forgetting for a minute that I didn't care.

"His parents founded this camp, but they

retired last year," she answered in her wheezy voice. "His sister wanted to run the camp, but he won it in a court battle."

A court battle! Against his own sister? I already didn't like this guy. And you should have seen him. He was wearing bright Hawaiian shorts and a green polo shirt, stretched across his potbelly. Plus, he wore brown socks and sandals! The best part was his hair—he was almost totally bald, but he combed like three strands of hair across the top of his head to hide it. Who did he think he was kidding?

"I want to welcome back all the regular campers and extend a hearty howdy-do to the new recruits. I hope you'll all become members of our Camp Slumbering Pines family!" The regulars all cheered when he talked about them, and I could see Frank's new friends slapping him on the back when Creeley said howdy-do.

"But the best part about being here this summer is that you kids will witness the dawn of a new era for Camp Slumbering Pines," Creeley went on.

I mean, did this guy talk like a commercial or what?

"Deeper in the woods, beyond the regular campsites," he continued, "we're building an all-new summer facility. There will be brand-new cabins, with carpeting and air conditioning. We're building an Olympic-sized pool, and best of all, Camp Slumbering Pines will become a family camp! You and your parents will be able to have long weekends together when they join our summer community at the special family rate."

There was a smattering of applause—at first. People seemed to like the idea of a swimming pool, and *I'd* sure like any camp with air conditioning and carpeting. But when he said it was becoming a family camp, I heard everybody gasp.

"That is the lamest thing I've ever heard," Linda complained.

"Why can't he just leave stuff the way it is?" Rebecca whined. "I'd rather deal with the outhouse than have my parents here on weekends."

"He's just doing this to get loads of new business," Linda added. "That greedy pig."

I don't know, it sounded okay to me. Although I wasn't sure why anyone would leave the city just to sit around in a condo in the woods.

"Well, I'm sure you're all thrilled," Mr. Creeley said, laughing a little nervously. A few people clapped politely. "But now, the moment you've all been waiting for. The camp legend, told this year by Tom Bowman!"

An excited hush fell over the whole camp. Frank's counselor, the guy with the ponytail, got up and stood in front of the campfire.

"He's sooooo hot," someone said behind me.

"Oh, my gosh, I hate when they tell this story." Rebecca giggled nervously.

Tom held up his hands, and everyone was totally silent.

"For those of you who don't know, it's only fair to warn you," he began, in a grave voice. "The name of this place is Camp Slumbering Pines. But to those who know the legend, it will always be...*Camp Sasquatch*."

I heard a few giggles, but I was starting to feel seriously freaked out. That funny feeling was back, as if someone or something was watching me. I shivered and hugged my knees to my chest.

It's just a dumb story, I told myself. But something was feeling mighty strange.

"Sasquatch is another name for Big Foot, the creature that roams the woods of the Pacific Northwest," Tom went on. "They travel in bands, almost always remaining mysteriously out of sight. Some say they're a kind of ape. Scientists speculate that the creatures may be the missing link—part ape, part human. Leftover cavemen that refused to be civilized and hid in the hills for thousands of years.

"Before there was ever a camp here, there were loggers—men who stayed out in the woods for months. Isolated from regular society, braving the elements to fill the demand for lumber. They were tough men, and not much scared them. But in the summer of 1924, an event occurred that terrified these tough men so much, they abandoned their camp and never returned."

Tom pointed out across the darkening hills, where a crescent moon was beginning to rise.

"The loggers were working near a ravine, just east of here, when several huge creatures walked out of the woods. They were at least ten feet tall and covered with matted hair. But they had almost human faces—except for their massive, flesh-ripping teeth. The loggers retreated. But one of the creatures picked up a huge log— one that was too heavy even for several men to lift—and threw it across the ravine, as far as the length of a football field. The men fired at the creatures, and one of them stumbled. It had been shot!"

"*Bang!*" the oldest boys' bunk yelled, right on

cue. Everybody squealed, but then quieted down right away.

I'm telling you, if I was at home, watching this on TV, I probably would have thought it was corny. But out there? In the dark woods? You could almost see those big hairy ape-guys standing just outside the firelight.

"The creature stumbled a few feet, then fell down the ravine. The other creatures retreated to the woods, confused and terrified. But when the loggers got to the edge of the cliff to look at the wounded beast...*it was gone.*"

Tom looked out at us, meaningfully.

"The loggers thought they had scared off the creatures, and they celebrated that night. They sat around a campfire like this one, and drank and partied and fired their weapons into the sky. Then they went off to their cabins and fell asleep.

"But the Big Foot weren't scared off. They were angry. They returned that night, and the men in the logging camp cowered as their cabins were bombarded with rocks. The Big Foot were stronger than bears, craftier than raccoons. They didn't let up all night. The men shot at the Big Foot whenever they got the chance. Each time, the monsters would retreat for a few minutes...then they would return, pelting the cabins endlessly."

"Didn't the loggers run out of ammunition?" a kid asked. She was clinging to her friends. In fact, the whole bunk looked like a little knot of terrified campers.

Tom nodded gravely. "They did run out," he admitted. "And they thought they were totally done for. The Big Foot retreated for a minute, and the loggers thought they were getting ready for the big kill.

"But then the sky began to lighten, and the men realized the sun was rising. And the Big Foot didn't attack again. By the time the sun came up, the Big Foot had completely disappeared."

"But what happened to the loggers?" another kid asked in a quavery voice. It was the question we all wanted to ask, even me. Tom shook his head.

"It was too late for some of them. They went insane from the terror. One man's hair turned completely white that night. They all abandoned the camp, and none of them ever returned to the woods."

Tom shook his head and paced back and forth slowly.

"Over the years people returned to the area, but they were always very careful never to walk alone in the woods. We tell you guys this story so you'll understand that you can never, *never* go out alone. You never know when you'll run into a Big Foot. Even now, every once in a while, you can hear one of them howling in the woods."

Tom stopped talking and narrowed his eyes, listening carefully.

No one moved.

Then we all heard it.

A desolate howl, from deep in the woods.

I knew it. The Big Foot were back, and they were out for revenge!

4

Up Close and Personal

"Ha, ha, Tom," Linda yelled brazenly. Everybody was squealing and screaming and grabbing on to each other, but she was cool as a cucumber. "We know that's just some counselors hiding in the woods and trying to scare us."

She was probably right, of course. At least that's what I told myself as I sat huddled in the darkness.

But when I looked around, I saw a counselor with every bunk.

And Tom was still standing in front of the fire. I couldn't tell if he was really scared or just pretending he was. Anyway, the other girls were giggling and nudging each other by now.

"Ooooh, I've got chills," Rebecca giggled. I decided I was just being ridiculous—*again*. What was up with this place? It seemed that I was constantly getting spooked by nothing!

By now it was truly dark out. Heidi got us all

together and we went back up the trail. In case you were wondering, a crescent moon doesn't make much light, and as soon as we were out of sight of the campfire, we were surrounded by an inky blackness that was darker than anything I had ever seen in the city. The only light came from our flashlights, and mine was looking a little dim.

The other girls were still squealing and trying to scare each other, clinging together as they followed Heidi up the trail. I wasn't about to admit how scared I felt, so I stayed back a little bit.

I shone my flashlight on the ground, looking carefully for safe places to step. But after a few minutes, I realized I was getting separated from the rest of them.

"Hey, wait up!" I called, and tried to move faster through the trees. But stuff kept scratching at my legs, and my head got jerked back a few times when my hair got caught on branches. I suddenly realized why everyone else wore those high socks and baseball caps!

Meanwhile, I saw the line of flashlights moving farther away. I started running toward the lights, but it was no use. My feet wouldn't find the pathway. Nothing looked familiar, and the trees were reaching out to pull me back.

Calm down, I told myself.

I knew that if I panicked, I wouldn't get any-where. I had to be reasonable.

But just then, I got that really weird feeling again, as if something was watching me.

I took a deep breath and peered into the darkness. The flashlights of my bunkmates were totally gone. All around me it was pitch-dark, and the beam of my flashlight was getting weaker and weaker.

Something moved behind me.

I ran away from it and crashed into a tree. My flashlight dropped, then went out, leaving me in total darkness.

Nice move, Gina!

I leaned against the tree and tried to get my bearings. Then something brushed against my face! I swung wildly at it and ran a few feet. Now I was just standing there, all alone in the pitch-black woods. I began to back up, slowly.

I felt my back against something again. It felt kind of like the trunk of a tree except it was warm...and hairy...

I turned slowly, afraid of what I was about to see but unable to stop myself. Something told me to look straight up.

And there were the red gleaming eyes, the huge teeth, the massive body of...

Big Foot!

5

Would I Make This Up?

I let out a scream.

Oh, not just a scream. I was hollering bloody murder. I sounded like one of those girls in a horror movie, and I couldn't stop myself.

I turned away from the monster and ran blindly, not caring what I crashed into.

I stumbled and fell. But when I felt something brush my face in the darkness, I scrambled up again and kept running. I heard my feet thud in time with my pounding heart as I raced away from that creature.

Once or twice I thought it was in front of me again, and I changed direction and ran some more. I don't know where I thought I was going, but the woods finally opened up and I realized I was headed straight for my cabin!

The other girls were all standing around in a group, shining their flashlights out into the gloom. I let out a shriek and stumbled to my knees in front of them. I was exhausted. But I was finally safe.

They huddled around me, everyone talking at once.

"Oh, my gosh, where were you?" Rebecca asked. "You just disappeared!"

"Are you okay?" Stacey asked. "You've got some scratches on your face."

"Big Foot," I gasped. "I got lost and dropped my flashlight. I swear, I just saw Big Foot out there in the woods!"

As soon as I said it, I knew it was a mistake. Their expressions of concern faded instantly, turning to sneers of scorn. Especially Linda—she looked ready to laugh.

"Oh, really. Big Foot," she said sarcastically. "Are you sure it wasn't a rattlesnake?"

"I'm not lying," I protested. "I'm serious. I saw something out there! We should try to go back down to the barn. We have to get everyone together!"

"You know, we were really worried about you," Rebecca added, ignoring my warning. "It's bad enough you don't want to be friends with us, you don't have to be so mean," she said.

"Ugh, some people just always want to be the center of attention," Linda said, standing up and walking away.

It was no use. They weren't going to listen to me. Before I could say anything more, Heidi crashed out of the forest.

"It's okay, Ranger Rick turned up," Linda said. "She just took a little detour through the trees. And she thinks she saw *Big Foot.*" Man, I wished Linda hadn't said it that way. It sounded so stupid, especially now that I was out of the woods and safe. But Heidi just looked relieved that I wasn't lost.

"Gina, you gotta stick with the rest of the bunk," she said sharply. "Okay, everybody, the show's over. Let's all go inside and get some shut-eye." She stood next to me as the other girls filed into the cabin, eyeing me disgustedly.

"You know, it's just a story," she said to me, putting an arm around my shoulder. "The Big Foot legend is just something we tell every year. It's not true. Okay?" She patted my shoulder.

I felt totally stupid. I knew my story sounded crazy. But I also couldn't get the picture of that hairy creature out of my mind! I looked out into the forest, squinting to see if I could get a glimpse of those red glowing eyes. Then I reluctantly followed the others into the cabin.

After lights-out, I could hear my bunkmates whispering to each other, sharing secrets and giggling. I just stared out into the night, waiting for that thing to come back and get me. But part of me was also wondering if I had even seen it.

I mean, I had been really freaked out, all alone in the woods. Maybe I'd just panicked and thought I'd seen something. Still, I had this weird feeling that something was not quite right.

The next morning, everyone pretty much ignored me while we got dressed and went down to morning lineup. I wanted to scream at them, tell them that I *did* see something! But I figured I'd better keep my mouth shut. They didn't believe me anyway. And as long as they thought I was just a victim of an overactive imagination, at least they'd leave me alone. I needed time to think and figure out what to do.

When we had said the Pledge of Allegiance and were heading to the mess hall, Frank managed to catch up with me.

"I hear you saw Big Foot last night," he said, with a stupid grin on his face.

"Word travels fast," I commented. "I guess the whole camp knows."

"Pretty much," he assured me. "Heidi told Tom, and he told us. Some of the guys in my bunk are calling you 'Big Foot' now."

"Well, thanks for defending me, Frank. I'm only your sister!" I spat.

"Hey! Don't blame me!" Frank held his arms

out in mock surrender. "I'm not the one making up stories so I can go home."

We were just outside the mess hall door, and I turned away from him and stared at the shrubbery.

I'm not going to cry, I'm not going to cry, I'm not going to cry! I repeated to myself. That would have looked great, wouldn't it? Everyone hated me already. If they saw me crying and fighting with my own brother, I'd really look like an idiot.

I wanted to go home more than anything else, but I *knew* I hadn't invented that creature in the woods. And nobody believed me, not even my own brother.

"Hey, come on, Gina," he said behind me. "Don't get all upset about it. I know you want to go home."

"But I'm not lying," I finally said. I shivered as my encounter with the Big Foot replayed itself in my mind. "I really saw something."

He sighed and looked at me. My lower lip was trembling, in spite of my efforts to keep it still. I was exhausted, I was miserable, and I was desperate. I just looked back at him.

"You're not lying," he finally said. "I can always tell when you're lying, and you're not, are you?"

We don't have any kind of weird psychic twin link or anything, but he *can* always bust me when I'm lying.

"No, Frank, I am not lying!" I said firmly. "Okay? I saw something out there, and it was really weird. And I don't know what to do."

Now, this was a new thing for me. Admitting to my brother that I didn't know what to do. Or admitting to anybody that I didn't know anything, for that matter.

Frank seemed to be as surprised as I was. And he looked a little scared. It was easy to laugh if you thought Big Foot was just a story. But if it was real?

"So you really saw this thing, out in the woods last night?" he asked.

"I bumped into it, I saw it, and I took off running."

He nodded. "That's what I thought. You probably scared it."

"*Scared* it?" This was too much! "Frank, what are you talking about?"

"It was probably out in the woods by itself, and it didn't know you were there, and you didn't know it was there. You probably surprised each other!" He held out his hands as if his point was totally obvious. "Don't you remember? That time there was a mouse in the basement, and

Mom said it was more scared of you than you were of it?"

"Frank, that mouse was smaller than my big toe," I answered, exasperated. "I'm talking about a monster that's bigger than Dad!"

"Yeah, but the Big Foot doesn't know anything about people. It probably expected you to pull out a gun, like those loggers!" Frank nodded as though he definitely had it all figured out. "It was just a freak occurrence, and it's not going to happen again," he said confidently.

"I don't know," I said doubtfully. I wanted to believe what he was saying. But I wasn't sure. That...*thing* didn't look lost or scared.

"Think about it logically," Frank continued. "If these creatures were *really* dangerous, kids would be disappearing every summer, right? It would be all over the news, and they wouldn't be able to keep the camp open."

I had to admit, it made sense. My parents checked out this camp really well before they sent us here, and they would have uncovered any stories of missing campers.

"Okay, you're probably right." I nodded in agreement. "So I'm okay. They're not out to get me or anything."

"No. You're safe." He patted me on the shoulder, and we started to walk into the mess hall.

"Hey, Sasquatch!" one of the little kids in the junior bunks piped up as soon as I walked in.

"Great, the whole camp has a new name for me," I moaned.

"Well, at least you're safe from the Big Foot," he added. He headed over to his buddies, and I went to my lonely spot at my bunk's table.

Somehow, I made it through the day. The rest of the girls in the bunk warmed up a little, after a few activities. The woods didn't look so scary in the daylight, and Frank had convinced me that I was safe anyway. So I put the whole problem out of my mind and tried to enjoy some of the stuff we were doing.

It turns out I'm pretty good at arts and crafts, for one thing. This counselor named Betty was showing us how to make friendship bracelets— you know, where you tie a bunch of needlepoint thread to a safety pin and make a rope out of knots, and it makes a cool pattern.

I picked it up pretty quickly, and I made a little rope long enough to go around my wrist. Meanwhile, Miss Know-it-all Linda couldn't even get hers started.

"Why can't we just go fishing or something?" she complained, flipping her blond hair over her shoulder angrily.

"Well, I guess you'll go fishing another day,"

Betty told her. Linda shrugged and stuck her safety pin in her pocket. Then she lay back in the grass and stared at the sky.

"I think mine's done," I said, handing it to Betty.

"Hey! This is really good," she said, holding it up so the others could see. "The knots are nice and tight, and the rows of color are even. You did great, Gina!" She tied it around my wrist, and the other girls looked at it.

"I like the colors you chose," Stacey murmured.

"Thanks," I said, shrugging. Then I pulled back my arm and went to sit under a nearby tree. Stacey followed me.

"Will you start another one for me?" she asked. "This one is all messed up."

I tied the threads around the safety pin for her, and she started working on another bracelet, but I didn't say anything else. I could see that she was messing up this one, too. But I didn't want to talk to her and tell her what she was doing wrong. She might think I liked her, or something.

I mean, the whole thing was kind of confusing. Stacey was left out of a lot of stuff because she's so sick and wimpy, right? And I was left out because they just didn't like me. So Stacey and I were supposed to be automatically best friends or something. It just seemed like a weird way to make friends.

Besides, Stacey was a nerd. *It's better to have no friends than a nerdy friend,* I said to myself. Although that sounded kind of stupid.

And anyway, if I got friendly all of a sudden, they might think I was weird. Like I can't make up my mind. And what if I were nice and they were just mean back to me? Then I'd really look like a fool, wouldn't I?

It was better just to sit here and concentrate on making another bracelet. I could send this one to my mom, along with a letter begging her to let me come help her with my Aunt Sarah.

How bad could some dirty diapers be?

Fortunately, the next activity was horseback riding. Those giant, snuffling horses were pretty intimidating at first. But once you're actually sitting on one, it's pretty cool. And I just had to follow along the trail behind Rebecca. No sweat!

By lights-out, I was getting used to being the odd girl out, and it wasn't bothering me too much. I decided that I was doing research. When I got back to civilization, I would write a book about all the girls at this camp and how creepy and nerdy they were. Then it would sell a million copies and everyone would read it and laugh at them.

Then it wouldn't matter that they didn't like me.

I twisted and turned in my bed. I just couldn't get myself to sleep!

Whoever said that nature is peaceful and quiet was lying. The woods are full of crickets, which I swear are louder than car alarms. Some of them go *creep-creep, creep-creep*, and some sound like *geeeeeeeeeee!*

And just in case you doubted it, owls really do sound like they're saying "Who? Who-who?" It's totally annoying.

I wished they would all just shut up so I could have some peace and quiet.

Finally I had to do something. I grabbed my flashlight (I had bought a new one at the canteen that day at lunch) and went out the back door, to the outhouse.

If I had thought about it twice, I probably would have been too scared to go. But I was sort of sleepy and groggy. And I was sure that Frank was right—the Big Foot just let me see him by accident.

Anyway, I got out there okay and it was no problem. I thumped the outhouse door behind me and started to walk back toward the cabin when I heard something behind me. Like a twig cracking. A twig that someone—or some*thing*— had stepped on.

I started and dropped my flashlight. Again. I swear, they make flashlights out of extra-slippery stuff. Fortunately, it was still switched on, and I picked it up.

Calm down, I told myself. *You're only ten steps from the cabin, so just walk.*

But Frank's reassurances suddenly seemed very far away. And so did the cabin. I got that prickly feeling on the back of my neck, as if I was being watched. It was the same feeling I'd gotten when I was unpacking.

Still, I took a deep breath and stepped forward. And that's when I felt something drop over my head. It felt like a rough, heavy blanket, woven out of dried grass and vines.

And I was trapped inside it!

6

Midnight Run

I felt myself being hoisted up on someone's shoulders—someone *very* huge, with *very* hairy shoulders.

Arrrgh! I tried to scream, but the shoulder was digging into my stomach, and all I could manage was a squeak. My heart was pounding a million times a second. I couldn't believe this was happening to me!

I felt myself moving, slowly at first, then a little faster. My abductor was jogging along through the forest, moving swiftly and surely through the trees. I couldn't see a thing, but the movements were smooth and confident. I wasn't weighing it down too much, that's for sure.

We must have traveled miles. I was struggling the whole time, thumping on its back through the thick net. But its arms were like steel around my legs.

Finally, I felt myself being lowered to the

42

ground. I rubbed my sore belly and breathed freely. The thick mesh of the blanket was still covering my face. Then it suddenly slipped away. I looked around me, blinking in the dim light.

I was in some kind of cave. But it wasn't dark. It was made of rock with light inside it—I think it's called phosphorescent light—that gave the cave an eerie glow.

The rock walls rose up majestically to high ceilings, almost like a church's. There were long stalactites that looked like columns.

As my eyes traveled down the walls of the cave, I noticed that the walls were covered with paintings. Cave paintings.

Some of them looked like the ones in my textbooks at school—crude outlines of animals with sticks for legs, and suns that looked like circles with spikes coming out. But the paintings gradually became more and more sophisticated and colorful.

It was as if the cavemen who drew the first paintings had gone on drawing them over thousands of years. And gotten better and better at it.

Pretty weird.

Finally, I turned slowly to face the giant creature that had brought me here. It looked like the one I had seen in the woods the night before.

It was really huge, more than seven feet tall. Long, matted, dark brown hair covered its body, even its face. But under all that hair, the face looked oddly human. Like a person who had let his beard grow all over his face.

Except the eyes. They were a piercing red, and they glowed in the shadows like a cat's eyes.

I looked down its giant, muscular body to its hands and feet. The hands had five fingers, like mine. The feet had four long clawed toes and a little fifth toe that didn't even reach the ground. It was a Big Foot, and I was alone with him, in the middle of nowhere.

My heart sank into my stomach as it opened its mouth, revealing a full set of huge, mossy teeth.

7

Big Foot Food

"I hope you were not made too uncomfortable by your journey." The creature spoke in a deep, gruff voice. "It is not my wish to harm you...yet."

Now I was really floored.

"You can talk?" was all I could think of to say. It bared its disgusting teeth in an expression that I think was supposed to be a grin.

"You would be surprised. There is much you can learn, hiding in the shadows just beyond one of your campfires." My heart pounded at the thought of this huge monster, sitting just outside the light of the campfire. Just a few feet away from me and the other kids!

"I heard them call you Gina," he went on, pointing a huge clawed finger at my chest. Then he pointed at himself. "You can call me Oak."

Okay. So it had a name. I was opening my mouth to say something—like "Nice to meet you, Oak, but I really don't want to be Big Foot food"—when I heard a rustling sound.

At least a dozen more Big Foot appeared from out of nowhere. I mean, they weren't there one minute, and the next, they were just growing up out of the rock formations. As they walked toward us, my heart sank even more.

Oak was a dwarf compared to these other creatures. Most of them were *twice* his size. They were fourteen feet tall—taller than a basketball hoop!

"I am the youngest of our colony," Oak explained, seeing that I had noticed the size difference. "I am only fifty."

"Oh, you're just a kid," I couldn't help saying.

"I was sent to meet you last night, and to capture you today," he continued. "It was thought that I would be the least frightening."

"I don't see why that was necessary." An even deeper, gruffer voice objected. I looked over at the group. The biggest one, with the darkest fur, was glaring at me. "These—*people*—certainly don't spare *our* feelings." He moved in closer and peered at me. "Why don't we just make an example of this one?"

"We agreed!" Oak responded, moving toward me and standing between me and the king Big Foot. "Let me tell this one the story and then give her a chance to change things. If she fails, then we can take action against the Humans."

The giant guy backed off, grumbling, but not before he shot me one more nasty look. I almost wanted to stick my tongue out at him, but he could probably have crushed me with one hand. I looked nervously at Oak, wondering what the heck he was talking about.

"Come here," he said, crooking a giant finger at me. I walked toward the cave paintings where he was standing.

"Here we are," he said, pointing out a picture of dense trees in a forest.

As I looked closer, I could make out Big Foot creatures like him and his family, their red eyes peeking out between the trees.

"We live in the forest. Long ago, there used to be Humans that we made contact with. They called us Sasquatch."

He pointed to another picture, showing tiny people with the giant Big Foot. "Native Americans," I said.

"But about a hundred and fifty years ago, other Humans came and made the ones we knew go away. They gave them diseases and moved them from their homes. We did not trust these new Humans, and we stayed away."

"How come?" I asked indignantly. He moved

his finger along to another picture on the wall.

"This was the Great Battle," he said. "It was before I was born. The one we call Mica was my age then, and he was curious. He convinced some of the others to go with him to meet the Humans who cut down the trees."

"The loggers," I whispered, recognizing the old camp legend. In the picture, the humans were holding massive guns and the Big Foot were running away.

"Loggers." Oak nodded. "The Humans fired their guns and chased Mica and the others away. One of them fired again, and hit Mica on the arm. He still has the scar."

I looked back at the group. The biggest, meanest one, the one who was so eager to rip me open a few minutes before, rubbed his arm as if the memory still hurt.

"In anger, some of our colony went back to scare away the Humans—"

"By bombarding their cabins with rocks all night," I finished his sentence for him. "Three of them disappeared!"

Oak shook his head. "This is what you call exaggeration. They ran back to the city without their friends. We did not harm them." He looked at the picture again. "We didn't want to hurt anyone. But we may have to now."

"What are you talking about?" I asked.

Oak got an angry, wild look in his eyes as he pointed to the next painting. There were the trees again, with the Big Foot hiding in them. But the trees were being mowed down by big yellow machines.

Tractors. Bulldozers. Construction machines, drawn right there on the wall.

"These things are worse than people with guns," he said fiercely. "We have tried to destroy them when they are at rest, but new ones always appear. They invade our home. They rip out trees. The other animals flee, but there are few places we can go. We cannot stand for this. This is where we live!" He turned to me.

"There is a strange thing that has been happening to us lately," he whispered. "A strange, shadowy, dark feeling that haunts us. It won't let us retreat into the wilderness. It drives us closer to your camp, and it led us to you. You have to stop this destruction."

"Me? What am I supposed to do?" I objected.

"You stop them from building. You make them leave us alone," he said solemnly.

"Oh, great. Why don't you just ask me to grow horns and a tail?"

Me and my big mouth.

My mom always says it's going to get me in

trouble, and she's right. I was so angry that they had asked me to do this impossible task, I forgot that I was talking to huge, hulking creatures that could rip the flesh off me in a single bite.

"That is enough," Mica hissed in his hoarse voice. "This one will not help us. We will let the Humans know how serious we are by keeping this one here and destroying her if necessary. A few more missing campers, and no Humans will ever come near here again."

The huge, matted creature moved slowly toward me. I could feel its hot breath on me.

I backed up, wishing I hadn't said anything.

His red eyes gleamed, and his teeth clicked together hungrily as he moved closer...and closer...

8

Day of Terror

I was about to let out a shriek when Oak suddenly scooped me up and tossed me over his shoulder again. He was in such a rush to get me away from Mica, he didn't even bother with his woven net, and I could see the other Big Foot gathering together and shouting after him as he ran out of the cave.

I twisted around on his shoulder, pushing my hair from my face, trying to get a good look around me. The sky was just getting light, a sickly bluish gray that let me see a little of the surroundings. I could make out the dim outlines of the hulking yellow construction machines— the same ones in the cave painting.

They must be building the new camp right over those caves, I thought. *No wonder the Big Foot are mad.*

Still, I didn't see what I was going to be able to do to help. Especially not when I was bouncing uselessly along on the back of a Big Foot.

I pounded on Oak's back again, trying to get him to put me down. Those creatures had been ready to eat me! I didn't want him taking me away for his own private picnic. I'd rather find my way home alone.

Finally, we got to my cabin. My flashlight was still glowing weakly where I had dropped it, hours earlier. The world did a somersault as he heaved me off his shoulder and placed me on the ground.

"I am sorry they got so angry," he said. "They promised me they would leave you alone while I told you our story, but they still remember the Great Battle with rage. I was not born, so all I know is the story. But they saw."

"Well, I don't see how I'm supposed to help you," I said. "There's nothing I can do about the construction. I'm only eleven. Why don't you kidnap someone who can actually do something about it?"

"You are the one who can stop it. Everyone in the Zone knows this is true," Oak told me.

"Zone? What zone? What are you talking about?"

"The Shadow Zone. It is the place we come from. We returned there after the Great Battle, and most of the time your camp is not even visible to us. But your machines weakened the barrier between our world and yours. And, all of a sudden, your camp appeared."

"Wait a minute." I shook my head. This wasn't making any sense at all! "You didn't know where our camp was, and then you found it?"

"No." Oak looked kind of frustrated, like he was trying to figure out how to explain it to me. "Look. You see that we are standing on this hill, right?"

"Right." That much I knew.

"And here is the set of three trees standing together, and there is the big flat rock."

"Okay, yeah, I see that," I agreed.

"Well, when we're in the Zone, the hill is here, and the trees, and the rock. But your cabin is not. Where we stay, there are no Humans. And that is how we like it."

"So, the Zone is *this* place, only without the cabins, and without the camp?"

"Yes."

I thought about that one for a second. "So it's like a parallel universe?" I was trying really hard to understand. But it's tough to concentrate when Chewbacca is staring you down.

There was one thing about his story that still didn't make sense, though.

"But if you guys walk around most of the

time without even seeing us, and without us seeing you, why do you even care if we do the extra construction?"

Oak threw his hands up in the air. He looked exasperated, like my mom when I don't understand a math problem that she's explained fifty times already.

"Humans are destroying our forest, our home. But even worse, your machines are threatening our cave—and the barrier between your world and the Shadow Zone. You Humans must never enter the Zone. You must never even come near. We will not be forced to live among our enemies."

I pictured the Big Foot trying to scrunch into seats on the Metrobus. Then I pictured one of them reaching over and having the bus driver for a snack. I shuddered.

"We will not let it happen," Oak went on. "You must stop the construction, Gina, or disaster will strike."

"Oak, I don't even know what you're talking about. How am I going to stop—"

Oak held up a hand. Or paw.

"I am trying to help you as much as possible. I am doing my best to keep the others from attacking the camp. You have some time. Now stop the construction!"

I shook my head, not knowing what to say, and Oak melted silently back into the trees. The last thing I saw was his red eyes, and then he was gone. I picked up my flashlight and crept back into the cabin.

It felt so weird to be back in my bed after what had happened. There was no way I was going to get any sleep, that's for sure.

I lay there, thinking of the cave paintings and the huge creatures that drew them. I turned the ideas over and over in my head, trying to figure out if there was any way I could stop the construction.

Soon the sun was streaming into the cabin, onto my face. As the other girls started waking up and stirring in their beds, I realized I hadn't gotten a wink of sleep all night.

"I woke up last night," Stacey said quietly as she sat up in her sleeping bag. "I didn't see you in your bed."

"I just got up to go to the bathroom," I answered innocently.

But she was looking at me strangely. We heard reveille blasting over the PA system from the mess hall, and she shrugged and started combing her thin brown hair.

I got up and brushed my teeth and splashed water on my face, trying to clear my confused brain. *You have to stop the construction*, Oak's voice insisted over and over in my imagination. I had a feeling if I didn't do something, the Big Foot were going to freak out. But I didn't know what they wanted me to do!

I managed to pull Frank aside again after morning line-up. I could hardly believe the whole story myself, but I had to tell him. It wasn't just a freak thing! The Big Foot meant business!

Frank looked terrified as I filled him in on the events of the night before. How Oak had picked me up and carried me out to the construction site. Where their caves were. How Oak knew the story of the angry loggers.

"They took you away?" he asked, incredulous.

I nodded.

"And they want something from us now?" Frank asked in a worried voice.

"They want me to stop the construction of Mr. Creeley's new camp!" I told him. "I don't know what to do!"

"Don't worry! I'm not going to let them take you away again," he said fiercely. "I won't leave you alone."

My eyes almost bugged out of my head. I mean, this is Frank we're talking about. My twin brother. The guy who liked to tie my sneakers together and short-sheet my bed every chance he got.

All of a sudden, he was Mister Protective.

"We'll figure out something," he assured me.

I looked at him. He's big for an eleven-year-old, wiry and tall and strong. But he was dinky compared to Oak. How was he going to keep me safe? Still, just knowing he was there made me feel a little better. I managed a wan smile.

"All right," he said, punching my arm lightly. "Now go get some chow. We're going to need all our strength!"

I forced down a couple of pancakes and a cup of bug juice, wishing I could get my hands on some of the coffee the counselors were drinking.

After breakfast, Heidi lined us up outside.

"We're playing softball with the boys' bunk," she announced, and the rest of the girls squealed.

I was just glad Frank was going to be near me for the rest of the morning, and he grinned happily as Tom made the same announcement to his bunk.

We walked to the playing field in two lines. Heidi and Tom walked ahead of us, sort of strolling along together.

Oh, gross, I thought. *Is that why they had our bunks play softball together? What is this, a camp or a dating service?*

Meanwhile, the girls from my bunk were being just as sickening.

"Do I look okay?" Linda asked anxiously.

"I didn't brush my hair," Rebecca moaned.

Oh, boy. I realized with a flash that these nature girls were scared of boys! They could stick worms on fishhooks and pick up snakes, but they became terrified when a male member of their own species was around. I had to laugh! They definitely needed my help.

Heidi and Tom broke us up into teams and we started playing. After an awkward first few innings, everyone started loosening up a little, and the girls stopped pretending they didn't know how to play.

I got a couple of good hits, and one of Frank's bunkmates yelled, "Go, Sasquatch!"

Frank whacked him, but I actually thought it was kind of funny. He didn't mean it in a nasty way, and they *were* good hits.

In the bright sunshine, the horror of the night before seemed really far away. Frank and I sat together on the bench, waiting to get up to bat again, and I started to relax a little. Big mistake.

Linda hit a pop fly out to left field, where Stacey was waiting to catch it. She held up her skinny little arm, wearing a mitt the size of her head, and missed the ball. It bounced behind her into the trees, where three or four other kids chased it.

I was laughing a little and telling Frank what a wimp Stacey was when suddenly there was a huge commotion. Everyone was gathered in the outfield, staring at something on the ground.

We got off the bench and hustled over there to see what was going on. They were all looking down at the ball.

"The ball went into the trees," Stacey explained.

"So we were going to look for it," Stephen McKean continued for her. "But someone threw it back out at us. But there wasn't anyone in the woods!"

I couldn't help myself. I reached down and gingerly picked up the ball.

There was a set of teeth marks in it, and a big chunk was missing. Someone—or something— had taken a *bite* out of the softball!

9

Creepy Creeley

"All right, all right," Heidi yelled, pushing through the other kids to get to us.

"What's going on?" Tom wanted to know. He looked at the softball in my hand, then around at everyone else.

Rebecca burst into hysterical tears and pointed at the ball. "Something...she's got it...threw it back..." She sobbed, clutching Heidi's arm.

Heidi grabbed the ball and inspected the bite mark. Linda told her what had happened in more understandable English. The guys from Frank's bunk were just standing around looking really uncomfortable.

"Well, looks like somebody's trying to scare you guys," she said, laughing.

But when she handed the ball to Tom, I caught a look of uneasiness between them.

"And it's working," Tom added. He was laughing too, but he glanced anxiously into the woods when he thought we weren't watching.

Funny thing about teenagers and grown-ups—they think kids can't tell when something's bothering them. But it was clear to me, at least, that the two counselors were pretty nervous.

Rebecca looked up at Tom for reassurance, though, and he patted her on the shoulder. She sniffled a few times and stopped crying.

"Come on, you guys, let's get back to the game. Tom has an extra softball in his bag," Heidi ordered, corralling us back toward the infield.

"Do you think that was a message for you?" Frank asked me anxiously as we returned to our spot on the bench. "Like, they're reminding you that they're out there?"

"I think so," I said. "I'd better do something fast. I've got an idea, though."

"What is it?" Frank wanted to know.

It was a pretty stupid plan, but it was the best I had been able to come up with all morning. And it was all I had.

"I'm going to go to Mr. Creeley," I sighed. "I'm going to tell him the truth. It's such a crazy story, he's got to believe it. Who would make up such a thing?"

"I don't know much about Creeley," Frank said. "I hear he's kind of a jerk. But I can't think of anything better."

Just then, another kid from Frank's bunk hit a long shot to the outfield. Stacey grabbed for it, but when it went past her she just watched it settle near the woods.

"Stacey, go get the ball!" Heidi shouted.

Stacey looked dubiously at me, and I shrugged.

Marc, the other outfielder, walked slowly over to the ball with her. They grabbed it quickly and ran back to open ground.

The rest of the game was like that—everybody kept to the infield as much as possible, and all the batters carefully tapped the ball so it wouldn't go too far. It didn't make for a very exciting game, but no one was looking for any more excitement.

I guess it would have looked pretty funny, all of us timidly tiptoeing around the field like that, if you didn't know what we were afraid of. As far as I was concerned, the woods were full of those red, staring eyes from the paintings. And I wasn't going to get any closer to them than I had to!

The game finally ended—nine innings and no runs—and we went back to the mess hall for lunch.

Everyone was pretty quiet.

I didn't have much of an appetite, that's for

sure. I munched on a corner of my grilled cheese sandwich and then asked to be excused. Heidi gave me permission distractedly, and I ran around to the back of the building, to Mr. Creeley's office.

It was pretty fancy, compared to the rest of the camp. The office building was made of the same mosquito netting as the other buildings, but the wooden beams and floors were painted a clean, fresh white.

Just outside the door, there was a table with a Plexiglas box on it. I looked at the box carefully. There were little white buildings, a tiny pool, miniature plastic trees....It looked like a scale model of the plans for the new camp.

I shook my head and went inside.

"Mr. Creeley?" I asked, letting the door close behind me. He looked up from his desk, but didn't smile. He was talking on the telephone, complaining that someone had delivered too much food to the camp.

"I've got to store all of this," he yelled. "Where am I going to put that many loaves of bread? I specifically ordered less than that!" He held up a finger to me. "Just a minute," he mouthed.

I looked around. The office was pretty neat. I guessed that he had had it repainted, since this was his first year as camp director. There were a couple of filing cabinets and a folding chair. On a card table by the door was a pile of framed pictures. They were old and dusty. The photographs must have hung on the office wall before it was repainted. But the way the pictures were carelessly piled up made me doubt that he planned to hang them up again.

There was one picture of an older couple. They looked rugged, like the people in the L. L. Bean catalogs, and they were smiling. The guy looked sort of like Mr. Creeley, only older, and I figured they were his parents. They were standing proudly in front of the mess hall.

There was another picture, with the same couple looking much younger, and two kids— Mr. Creeley and his sister, I guessed. His sister looked athletic and had a big grin, like her parents'. Mr. Creeley was kind of pudgy, and his smile was lopsided and fake-looking. He stood off to the side a little. Everyone was holding fishing poles. Everyone had a big bunch of dead fish, too—except little Mr. Creeley. He just had the fishing pole, squeezed tight in his fist as if he'd like to break it.

"Can I help you?" Mr. Creeley interrupted my thoughts. I looked up and cleared my throat nervously.

"I'm Gina Giardelli," I introduced myself. He

just stared at me, and it made me feel pretty uncomfortable. "I'm new this summer?"

"Right, the twins," he said, nodding.

Normally I would have said something about that. I hate it when Frank and I are lumped together, as if we're just one big person. But I didn't have time to waste, and I wanted to start off on the right foot with this guy.

"I have something I have to tell you," I said, sitting on a metal folding chair. "There's something going on, and I think you're going to have to think about this new camp you're building."

He just stared at me some more, so I launched into the whole story. I told him that I had seen Big Foot on my first night at camp, but that nobody believed me, and that I didn't think it was possible myself. But then, the next night, Oak came and got me himself and showed me the cave under the construction site, with all the paintings.

I told him about the Big Foot's demand that the construction be stopped or the creatures would start picking off campers. And then I told him about the bitten softball.

As I wound up my story, I took a deep breath. I didn't know how Mr. Creeley was going to take it.

To my surprise, his mouth widened into a smile.

"Gina," he said, shaking his head. "You really want to get out of here, don't you?"

"What?" I asked. "That's not what I'm talking about. The Big Foot—"

He held up a hand and shook his head again, as if he knew what I was going to say. "It's no secret. Your parents told me this was your first time away from home, and they said you'd be apprehensive. And Heidi told me about your little 'sighting.'" He held up his fingers like little quotation marks when he said "sighting" in a really condescending tone. I rolled my eyes and tried to say something again.

"And I understand you don't get along with your bunkmates, and that must be tough. But to make up these stories!" He gave a little laugh. "To tell you the truth, I would have expected something a little more believable than this!"

"Mr. Creeley, you don't understand. I'm not making this up!" I objected.

"I'm not sending you home, young lady," he said, more sternly. He leaned forward and rested his beefy elbows on the desk and nodded at the big black telephone.

"This is the only phone in the camp, and I'm the only one who uses it. And I'm not calling

66

your parents! They paid good money for you to be here, and I'm going to see to it that you stay put. I'm not about to lose the money your parents paid for you and your brother!"

I sat back, defeated. There was no getting through to this guy.

"And as for the new camp I'm building, you're just being silly to try to stop me. Why, you of all people should appreciate what I'm trying to do here!" He got up and led me out the door, to the model camp.

"Look. Here are the air-conditioned buildings. There's going to be a television in every bunk! Plus outlets, so you can use your hair dryers and curling irons."

His pudgy finger moved over to the tiny pool. "This baby is going to be heated. No more icy mornings in the lake!" he exclaimed proudly. "Now, you and all your little friends in the city...you'd love a camp like that, wouldn't you? You'd *beg* your parents to send you to a place like that!"

I thought about it for a minute, staring at the fancy little plastic camp. He was wrong about me and my friends—if we wanted all the stuff he was showing me, we had it all right there in the city. There was a pool at the YMCA, and I had electricity in my house! If anyone wanted to get away from all that, why would they go to an exact replica of their home, only out in the woods? It was totally stupid.

But he was convinced it was a great idea, so maybe I was wrong. Maybe he could fill up the camp with city dwellers looking for a little bit of Nature Lite. But something about his whole attitude really made me want to barf.

I swear, if you looked really closely at his eyeballs, you would have seen little dollar signs in the pupils. He didn't really care about Camp Slumbering Pines, the camp his parents had built. He probably hated it since he was a kid. He just wanted to tear it down and make it different.

Anyway, it was obvious that I wasn't going to convince him to stop the construction. Not with my crazy story and no proof.

"Okay, I'm sorry I wasted your time," I said. "I'll try not to make any more waves."

I turned to go, but something caught my eye. It was a hunk of rock shoved against the leg of the table, to steady it. There was a line of paint on it. I squatted down to get a better look, but I knew what it was.

It was a piece of the Big Foot's cavern wall!

10

Brain Power!

"Mr. Creeley!" I whirled around to face him. "This piece of rock—it's from the underground cave! You know all about it!"

He looked at the rock, then back at me. He sighed and rolled his eyes.

"Yes, so, I've been in the cave," he admitted. "I was surveying the area, and I stumbled on the entrance. But before you go thinking it's some kind of ancient artifact, I can tell you it's no big deal. I had the paint analyzed at a lab. It's recent."

"So what does that prove?" I wanted to know.

"It proves that the paintings weren't actually made by cavemen," he said triumphantly. "Some local yokel snuck in there and slapped some paint on the walls just to make trouble." He laughed a little and shook his head. "Boy, if I hadn't been so quick-thinking, those stupid natural history groups might have found out about it and really made some trouble. They would have been all over me!"

"But Mr. Creeley, the Big Foot painted that cave! This proves what I've been saying. Why won't you believe me?"

Now Mr. Creeley wasn't smiling at all.

"I don't know what you hope to gain by ruining my plans for the new camp," he said in a cold, mean voice. "But you are not going to stop this construction." He narrowed his eyes at me. "Do you understand?"

I understood, all right. I understood that this direct approach wasn't going to work with Mr. Creeley. I still had to stop the construction, but I also had to make him think I was just bluffing the whole time, so he wouldn't suspect anything.

"Well, I guess I can't fool you, Mr. Creeley," I said, smiling weakly. "You just aren't going to send me home, are you?"

He relaxed a little and grinned. I don't know what a wolf looks like, but I have a feeling it looks a lot like Mr. Creeley when he grins.

"What a dumb stunt," I said, slapping myself on the forehead. "It was just a joke....I sure miss my MTV!"

"I thought you'd see it my way. And I don't want to hear any more nonsense from you,

Gina." He slammed the door to his office behind me. I went back to the mess hall. I was feeling pretty hopeless.

The mess hall was usually pretty loud, with everyone yelling and talking at once. But people had been talking about the softball incident, and they already knew about my close encounter story. I think they were all starting to wonder if it was true.

I sat down at my table. Stacey scooted over and leaned in close to my ear.

"I believe you now, and so does Rebecca," she whispered.

"Well, I don't," Linda insisted, from across the table. "I still think it's a stupid story."

Stacey ignored her. "The Big Foot *are* out there," she went on. "You were with them last night, weren't you?"

I looked around the table, and six pairs of eyes gazed back at me expectantly. I nodded. Then I told them about the caves, and the paintings, and the Big Foot's demands.

"I just went to Mr. Creeley's office and told him the whole story," I admitted. "He even knows about the caves, but he doesn't believe there's any reason to stop the construction. He doesn't care!"

"We should go out to the construction site

and lie down in front of the bulldozers and cranes," Stacey said suddenly. "They won't want to run us over, so they'll have to stop! My parents told me they used to do stuff like that in the sixties."

"That only works if someone else sees you do it," Rebecca objected. "Mr. Creeley will just pick us up and move us, and they'll go on."

"Besides, we can't sit out there forever," I agreed. "I mean, sooner or later, we'd have to go back to school, and they would just do it then."

"He's such an idiot," Linda complained. "He's got a whole camp full of loyal kids who love it the way it is!"

"He'll be able to pack a lot more kids in, with the new camp," I explained to her. "City kids. Plus their parents, on the weekends. I don't think he cares if they're loyal or not—he just wants a lot of them. And their money."

Linda shook her head, totally disgusted. "I've been coming here since I was a little kid," she said. "My two big sisters went here, and even my parents! Old Mom and Pop Creeley were the best. Now Henry wants to make it into some big resort."

"I saw pictures of them in the office," I said. "What happened to his sister?"

"Darlene Creeley? Oh, she's around. She's a

schoolteacher most of the year, and everyone always thought she'd take over the camp when Mom and Pop retired. But Henry hired himself a high-priced lawyer and somehow got the whole camp." She shook her head and looked at me. "I don't believe your stupid Big Foot story, Gina, but I *would* like to see Henry leave the camp alone."

By that time, lunch was over. Frank gave me a reassuring wink, and I waved back. Heidi led us back up the path, explaining that she had a counselors' meeting and that we'd be on our own for a little while.

"You're supposed to be writing home to your parents, so give me the finished letters when I get back," she said.

"But, Heidi, what about Big Foot?" Rebecca wanted to know, clinging to her arm.

Heidi sighed. "You guys, I admit it was pretty weird, what happened this morning. But it was just a joke someone played on us, okay? It doesn't mean there are monsters or goblins or werewolves out there."

That's easy for you to say, I thought to myself, trudging up the path behind them. *You didn't get carried off to Big Foot land last night!*

"Whoop!" Heidi said, stopping suddenly. "Nobody move!" Everyone else stopped, too. I don't know about the others, but my heart just about stopped beating. I thought Heidi had run into one of the creatures!

"Be real quiet. And look over there—what do you guys see?"

We peered into the woods, looking for the Big Foot. I didn't see anything but leaves and trees. No red glowing eyes, no big nasty teeth.

"Oh, it's one of those raccoons from last year!" Linda finally said, in a loud whisper.

"That's right," Heidi said. "I think this one is Hector." I looked where she pointed.

"That's the giant rat you saw the first day," Stacey giggled. Sure enough, I recognized the weird little animal that had run away from me when I put down my duffel bag. Only it was really cool-looking, when you weren't startled by it. It had a little band of black over its eyes, like a tiny bandit, and long, thick hair. Its tail had stripes on it like a cat's tail, but it was a lot thicker.

"What is it doing?" I whispered back.

"Washing its food," Linda told me. There he was, crouched over a little stream, dunking something in and moving it around in his tiny little paws.

"Ah—cheee!" Stacey gave a high-pitched sneeze. The raccoon looked up, then scampered off in the other direction. A second later, he was gone.

Heidi looked at us happily. "They're still there, guys," she announced. She turned to me as we walked up the trail. "We studied those raccoons all last summer, and the summer before," she explained. "Since they were babies. We got to know them so well, we even gave them names. They're not tame, though," she added, looking at me. "They're still wild animals, and we want to watch, not pet."

"No problem here. I'm not petting anything that doesn't have a collar and a leash," I promised. She laughed.

To my surprise, we were already at the cabin. That trail got shorter and shorter every time I walked it. Heidi made sure we were all safe in our bunk, and passed out paper and pens for letters home. Then she changed into a bathing suit and brushed her hair out carefully.

Oh, right, a counselors' meeting, I thought. *Wonder if Tom is going to be there?* She checked herself out one more time in her little mirror, then said good-bye and went down the trail again. I hoped she wouldn't get devoured on the way down.

I flopped onto my cot and hugged my pillow. The other girls sat around, looking thoughtful.

"Maybe we could do something so the construction machines just wouldn't work," Rebecca offered after a few minutes.

"Yeah, great idea, Gilligan," Linda said, squishing a beetle with her bare fingers. "We'll get the professor to invent something right away."

I smiled in spite of myself. Linda was a pain, but she was also pretty funny. And *Gilligan's Island* is one of my favorite afterschool reruns.

Suddenly, I heard a wheeze and a squeak from the bunk next to mine. I looked up, and Stacey was staring wide-eyed out the window behind me.

"Big Foot!" she squeaked.

I turned quickly as everybody screamed. There, in the dim shade of the trees outside the window, I could see a pair of bright eyes!

11

Brute Force!

Green eyes. And a not-so-hairy face.

"Frank!" I scolded him. My heartbeat was slowly returning to its normal pace. Everyone groaned with relief. Frank grinned and came in the door.

"Sorry," he said sheepishly. "Didn't mean to scare you."

"What were you doing out there?" I demanded. "You shouldn't be running around in the woods by yourself."

"Well, I wanted to make sure you were okay," he admitted.

"Aww," the other girls said, all at once. I glared at them. They were all piled together on Stacey's bed, staring at Frank as if he were a creature from Mars.

"Yo, cut it out," I told them.

"Frank, isn't Tom going to be mad you left?" Linda asked.

"He's at that meeting," Frank said.

"Okay, well, I'm okay, so you can run along home now," I said, trying to shoo Frank out the door. I mean, it was too weird watching my bunkmates moon over him.

"Wait, I gotta tell you what we saw after lunch," he said. "I think Big Foot has been back."

"*What!* What did you see?"

Frank sat at the foot of my cot. "As we headed back to our bunks, we passed the flagpole. You know, the flagpole? The tall, straight, metal thing we all stare at every morning?"

"Yeah, we know what a flagpole is," I said. Frank can sure drag out a story. "What happened?"

"Gina, I've never seen anything like it. The flagpole was all bent. Like a big zigzag!" He shook his head. "It was really weird."

"I've watched my dad weld metal like that," Linda broke in. "Someone could have just done it as a trick."

"But we would have heard the machinery," Frank objected. "We were playing softball nearby. And we just saw the flagpole this morning, at lineup—it would take a lot longer than a couple of hours to do that much work. And, I'm telling you, the zigzags looked like perfect right angles!"

"Why would the Big Foot do that?" Rebecca shook her head. "It doesn't make sense. Why would anyone bend a flagpole?"

"They're playing with our minds," Stacey said. "They're not just strong. They're smart, too."

I shivered. Stacey was right. These Big Foot weren't just dumb animals that relied on brute force. They were thinking creatures, and they could talk and reason just as well as we could. That made them even more threatening.

"Hey, campers!" Heidi called to us from the woods. She was coming up the trail!

"Oh, no!" I said, panicking. "If she catches Frank here, Big Foot is going to look like a pussycat."

"Come on, the back door!" Stacey pulled him to the other exit, by the outhouse. Everybody gathered in the doorway as he waved and disappeared into the woods.

"Bye, Frank!" Linda called out. Then she looked at me anxiously. "Do you think he'll be okay?"

Man. I mean, this was the same girl who could squish beetles with her bare fingers and put worms on fishhooks without batting an eyelash. Turned into lime Jell-O by the presence of a boy!

"I think he'll be okay," I assured her, though I wasn't sure myself. He looked awfully small, moving alone through the forest.

Heidi told us that her meeting had taken a lot longer than she had thought it would, because someone had played a trick. When one of the counselors walked out to the parking lot, he found that a car had been picked up and placed on top of another one!

"It took a bunch of us twenty minutes to roll it off. And the flagpole!"

"We know—" Linda started to say, but Rebecca clapped her hand over her mouth.

"She means, we know it must be a great story," Stacey said, thinking fast. Boy, she may not be able to move too fast, but that girl can think her way out of anything. "What happened to the flagpole?"

Heidi told us Frank's story, about the bent metal. "I don't know how they did it," she marveled. "I didn't even see burn marks on the pole. It's as if someone just bent it with his bare hands!" She shook her head, frowning.

"Anyway, it's nothing for you guys to worry about," she assured us, trying to sound like her regular, chipper self. "I'm sure Mr. Creeley will figure out who's responsible. The important thing is, nobody got hurt. It's all pretty harmless!" She gave a little laugh. "Now, who wants to go fishing?"

You know, if anyone ever tries to tell you that fishing is a sport, tell him to shut his mouth. Linda had to bait our hooks, of course, and we all sat by the river with our poles sticking out. And then we sat. And sat. And sat! I mean, what is the point?

There was a whole bunch of excitement when Linda caught a little silver fish. I felt really sorry for it, gasping for breath while its gills heaved on the side of its head.

"Too small to eat," she said, picking it up and staring it in the face. "Helloooo, Mister Fish. Would you like to give Rebecca a big kiss?" She held it out to Rebecca, who squealed and turned away.

"Linda, throw it back!" Heidi ordered. Linda finally did, and the fish swam away, probably feeling just as terrified as I had felt that night after Oak dropped me off at my cabin. And then we stuck our hooks back in the water and sat some more.

I guess, after a little while, it might have been nice. Just staring up at the trees and stuff, while Heidi told us what all the plants were and pointed out different birds. But I was thinking about the Big Foot, wondering if they were nearby. If they were watching us. If they were going to do anything to us. It's really hard to relax when you know there are ape-men hiding in the trees, waiting to make you into kid kebabs.

Nothing happened, though. We made it through the afternoon and dinnertime with no other incidents, and soon it was time for lights-out again.

"Do you think they'll come back tonight?" Stacey asked, propping up her little brown teddy next to her bed. The bear stared at her, goggle-eyed and stupid, as she snuggled into her hypoallergenic foam pillow.

"I don't know what they're going to do," I said truthfully. "It's not as though they ask me if I want visitors."

In fact, I was starting to doubt that I'd ever get a good night's sleep in this place. Every night so far, something popped out of the woods to scare me silly. Still, as I settled into my sleeping bag, I hoped everything would be okay. I mean, the Big Foot had given me their warning. They had to give me time to do something!

Everyone else fell asleep quickly, in spite of our totally scary day. I guess it's pretty tiring, being terrified all the time. In fact, I was just dropping off to sleep myself when I felt those red eyes boring through the back of my skull. I woke up with a violent shiver. I knew it wasn't a dream. A Big Foot was near. I pulled myself deep into my sleeping bag and rolled over slowly. Sure enough, Oak was sitting just outside the wall of the cabin, staring at me.

I stared back, the sleeping bag pulled up to my chin, and he gestured that he wanted me to come outside. I shook my head. *No way, mister.* Oak nodded and held something up for me to see.

Stacey's teddy bear!

But I was there the whole time! We all were! I was dozing a little, but I wasn't fast asleep at any point. How could he have snuck in without my hearing him?

I sat up and looked over at Stacey. She was snoring, wheezing a little in her sleep. And the bear was gone from its perch by her head. Oak was agile, and he moved completely silently. There was no telling what he'd do if I ignored him now.

I glared at him.

He lifted a claw and dragged it down the length of the screen by my bed, making a low, scratching sound. I watched, stock-still, while he slowly grasped a piece of the wooden frame of the cabin. A chunk of it came off easily in his hand. He moved his hand toward it again, still staring at me. He was ready to take the whole place apart!

"Stop it!" I hissed.

He motioned to me again, telling me to come outside. I thought about pulling my sleeping bag over my head and just ignoring him, but he pulled another hunk of wood off the frame. He tossed it over his shoulder, and I heard it land with a soft *thunk.*

If he wanted to kill me, he would have already done it, I reasoned to myself. *I may as well go hear what he has to say.*

"All right," I whispered.

I pulled myself out of my sleeping bag and grabbed my flashlight. Then I went out the front door, closing it quietly behind me.

He was sitting on the huge hunk of cement that we used as a step into our cabin. I just stood next to it and looked at him.

"Give me the teddy bear," I demanded, trying to sound tough.

"You have to listen to me first," he answered, holding the tiny bear in his huge hands.

"I don't have to listen to anything!" I whispered angrily. "What was with that stupid softball trick today? And the flagpole. And the car!"

"You didn't do anything to stop those machines," he answered. "They tore down more of the forest today. They aren't stopping!"

"I tried!" This was so frustrating! Why did Oak think I was going to be able to stop anything? "I went to Mr. Creeley. He doesn't care! He's going to build his camp no matter what any kid says to him."

"You have to try harder," was Oak's answer. "I didn't do any of that damage to the camp today. It was the others. I wanted to give you more time, but they are impatient. And I am starting to agree with them. I thought we could depend on you, Gina, but maybe they are right. You can't do anything!"

"Well, thanks for the news flash, you big dumb ape!" I snapped. "I *can't* do anything. I'm just a kid! And besides, I don't care about your stupid forest. I just want to go home!"

Oak's eyes got tiny and bright, like when you turn off an old television set. Then his eyes began to glow like two hot, angry coals. He stood up. I took a few steps backward. What had I been thinking? This was Sasquatch, not some substitute teacher I could just mouth off to!

Oak still held the teddy bear in one hand. With the other, he reached down and yanked the huge cement step out of the ground and tossed it into the woods as if it were made of cardboard.

He could toss *me* right into the forest too!

12

Toe Count!

"This is your last warning!" Oak said to me. Then he threw down the teddy bear and tore off into the woods. I didn't know whether to be relieved he was gone or worried that I had really made him angry. I picked up the little stuffed animal and climbed up into the cabin. It was tricky now that the cement step was gone.

I carefully placed the teddy bear on Stacey's pillow. She gave a little whimper, as if she was having a bad dream. I slipped back into my sleeping bag and curled up. I faced the outside and stared into the gloomy night. Did you ever notice how you can't close your eyes with your back to something scary? I was sure I wasn't going to get any sleep.

Then again, I hadn't slept at all the night before. In spite of my terror, I sank into a deep slumber almost immediately. But my dreams were full of ape creatures.

Instead of waking to reveille blasting over the PA system the next morning, I was jolted awake by Heidi's hollering from outside the cabin. We all dragged ourselves to the door. Heidi was standing where our front step used to be, her hands on her hips.

"Okay, you guys," she said. "These practical jokes have gone far enough! Does anybody know where our front step might have disappeared to last night?" She was really angry! But since none of the grown-ups at this camp were going to believe my Big Foot explanation, I just kept my mouth shut.

At morning lineup, Mr. Creeley managed to hang the flag on the bent flagpole, where it flapped limply at an odd angle. He was trying desperately to pretend everything was fine. But when we got to breakfast, it was obvious to everyone that *something* was wrong at Camp Slumbing Pines.

At each meal there's a designated waiter from every table. We take turns, and that day it was Linda's turn. She had to get the food and bug juice and bring it back for the rest of the table.

"You guys aren't going to believe this," she said in her flat, loud voice. She dropped a huge bowl and a plate on the table.

"Ugh, powdered eggs!" Stacey grimaced. "I can't eat that. It'll give me hives!" I peeked into the bowl. It looked like moldy, runny tapioca pudding, floating in a yellow puddle.

"It'll make me barf," Linda agreed. "You guys, feel the toast!"

We each grabbed a piece and groaned. The bread was so stale, it felt like hunks of rubber in our hands. We bent the toast into little tepees and rolled it into balls, but there was no way we would eat this garbage!

"Can I have your attention, please?"

We all turned to the front of the room, where Mr. Creeley was standing with his hands up. Everyone started booing at once. A couple of pieces of toast were flung at him.

"I don't blame you for being angry. This is all my fault," he said, giving us a smarmy smile. "I put in my regular food order, but the delivery people brought only half of what we needed. So we'll just have to make do until they get another shipment here!"

Something sounded awfully strange about his explanation. I turned it over in my mind, and then it hit me.

When I was in Mr. Creeley's office the day before, he had complained that too much food had been delivered! Now he was saying he didn't have enough? It didn't make sense!

I looked across the room at Frank and gestured to the back door of the cafeteria. He nodded. I excused myself and snuck out the door, where he was waiting.

"Creeley said he had too much food!" I blurted. Then I slowed down and explained the whole thing to Frank.

"Let's go check it out," he suggested, and we tiptoed around to the kitchen. Behind it was a metal shack and a giant refrigerator, where the food was stored.

The door of the refrigerator had been torn off and tossed aside. Giant bread loaves had been thrown out of the shack and lay moldering in the dewy grass. The ground was littered with smashed eggs, and the side of the building looked as if it had been used for target practice.

Smashed jelly jars, piles of flour blowing around like snowdrifts, dented cans of vegetables...it looked like a food-fight war zone!

"Whoa," I said. "Maybe it was just bears that did this."

"'Scuse me," a voice piped up behind me. Frank and I spun around.

"Stacey!" I said, angrily. "Why did you follow us out here?"

She pointed at the ground. Her tiny, skinny,

sneakered foot was inside the most humongous footprint I had ever seen.

"It's not a bearprint. Bears have five toes. This footprint has four. I bet the Big Foot did this!" she said, her gray eyes open wide.

"But why? Why would they break into our food supply?" Frank asked.

"They're angry, I guess," I said. Then I thought of something else. "Oak said the construction was destroying their habitat. Maybe their food supply is running out. They had to come here to get food. And when it runs out..."

We all looked at each other uncomfortably.

"Good thing I'm so scrawny," Stacey said, with a gulp. "They won't want to eat me!"

"Nobody's eating anybody," Frank said. He gave her arm a reassuring little squeeze. "I've got a great idea. I don't know why I didn't think of it before!"

"I'm all ears," I said, moving away from the empty refrigerator. It was giving me the creeps.

"We're all going on that canoe trip this morning, right? Well, when we get back, we'll make an excuse to call Dad."

"Mr. Creeley said he wouldn't," I objected.

"That's because you're such a troublemaker," Frank pointed out. "He won't mind if it's just me. I'm the *good* twin, remember?"

He was right, of course. Grown-ups always trust Frank! He was born with the natural ability to kiss up. But the first time they see me, they seem to know I'm going to be a problem...which makes it very difficult for me to get away with anything!

"Okay. But what are we going to tell Dad?" I wanted to know.

"We'll tell him about the Big Foot, and he'll come and do a news story on them."

"On Big Foot? Come on, Frank. He works for a news show, not a talk show. He'll never believe it!"

"Then we'll tell him about the cave paintings! Creeley said the natural history groups would care about them."

It sounded nutty at first, but the more I thought about it, the more I liked it. It fit in with what Stacey had said about the sit-ins her parents used to go to. We needed to get some attention focused on the construction site so Mr. Creeley wouldn't be able to build there!

"It's a great plan, Frank," I said, grinning. "Dad's going to love this!"

We snuck back into the mess hall and rejoined our bunks. Everyone was already lining up to go canoeing. We all trooped down to the water, where three or four of us got into each boat. We had to wear these totally dweeby orange life jackets. Mine fit snugly around my neck. I'm sure my face looked like a big daisy.

Still, I was feeling pretty good as we paddled out onto the river. Frank and I had a plan, so everything would be okay really soon. The trees reached up over our heads. When the river narrowed, they crossed over the water like a big, green canopy, and we floated along peacefully.

I could almost learn to like this, I thought, listening to the lazy buzzing of the insects and watching the trees roll by us. They began to roll a little faster as the river current picked up speed.

"Watch out for the tree!" I heard someone yell.

I sat up suddenly in our canoe, and it rocked violently. I grabbed on to the sides and looked up. At first, I couldn't see what was wrong. The branches were dipping down close to the water, but they were still way above our heads.

Then I saw Frank standing in a canoe up ahead.

Or was he dangling from the branch?

I couldn't tell what was happening exactly. But Frank was in trouble!

I squinted, trying to get a better look. All of a

sudden, a big, hairy arm reached out of the tree and grabbed Frank's shoulder.

My heart was beating a mile a minute. I had to help my brother, but I was stuck in this stupid canoe!

The kids in Frank's canoe held on to his legs. But before they could get a good grip, Frank disappeared into the trees!

13

Kidnapped!

Everything went crazy at once.

Some of the kids stood up in their canoes, then tipped over. Counselors jumped in after them, making sure everyone was okay as their little heads bobbed in the water. Other canoes bumped into the riverbank, where the kids clung to the branches and pointed to the spot where Frank had disappeared.

Tom was whacking at the branches, looking for him.

"I saw something grab him," one kid said.

"Did he fall in the water?" someone else wanted to know.

Everything was totally confused, and the current was stronger than we thought. As soon as we stopped paddling, the water carried us along to another part of the river. Some kids were crying, and some were just trying to get over to the banks again.

The counselors sprang into action. They got everyone out of the water and pulled the canoes up onto the shore.

"Move it! Get up on the dry ground. Everybody hold hands with your bunkmates, so we know we're all accounted for. *Now!*" Heidi yelled.

I guess this was where her yelling came in handy. I was kind of glad she was in charge. I, for one, felt totally numb. I couldn't believe I'd just watched my own brother get kidnapped. I think I was in shock.

As soon as we were all safely on the shore, half of the counselors hopped into canoes and paddled back upstream, calling Frank's name. But it was too late. I could have told them not to bother—he had disappeared without a trace.

The rest of the counselors led us back to our cabins and told us to stay put while they joined the search. As soon as they were out of sight, I jumped up and peered out into the woods.

"Where is he? What did they do with him?" I wanted to know. Now I was totally frantic. What if the Big Foot were out there, preparing for a Frank barbecue?

"What are we going to do?" Linda asked. "How are we going to find him?"

"*We?* I'm staying right here," Rebecca objected, clutching her pillow.

"Frank needs our help," Linda insisted.

"Hey!" I said, to shut them up.

They all looked at me, and I realized that for
once in my life I had no idea what to say next.
But looking at the ring of faces, I realized that
the other girls were all scared, and they wanted
my help. Most of them were willing to do whatever they could to help me, too. And I hadn't
even asked!

"Frank had a great idea before he disappeared," I said calmly. "He said he would tell Mr.
Creeley that he wanted to call my dad. Then he
was going to tell my dad to drive out here and
do a story. Now, Mr. Creeley is going to be busy
searching for Frank. I've got to get down to his
office and follow through on the plan! Maybe
then the Big Foot will see that we're doing something and let Frank go."

I stopped talking and looked at them. I
couldn't believe how much sense I was making!
Linda nodded.

"I think that's a good plan," she said.

"I'm going with you," Stacey squeaked.

"What?" This was too much. What was I going
to do with this little wimp trailing me?

"If anyone finds you, if you get caught, you

can say you were taking me to the nurse!" she insisted, her lips set in a pale, determined line. She was right, of course. It was an excellent cover.

"Okay," I said. "Let's go."

We made our way down the path and around the main building without meeting anyone. Once or twice we heard the shouts of the counselors calling to each other, but we stuck close to the buildings and no one saw us. Finally we got to Mr. Creeley's little white office.

"Okay," I told Stacey. "You keep watch out here."

I slipped in the door of the office, but not before I noticed the miniature camp. The Big Foot must have known what it was, because it was totally mangled. I got an awful chill as I stepped over the broken pieces and in the door.

I picked up the phone and dialed my home number. I really had to dial it, too—all the way out here in the sticks, they still had rotary phones! It took forever for me to get it right. My finger kept slipping out of those little holes, and the dial turned so slowly. I don't know how people managed before they invented the push-button kind. I finally got it right, and the answering machine picked up.

"You have reached the Giardelli residence." I

heard my mom's voice on the tape. She sounded so self-conscious! I just wanted to cry, I missed her so much. "Leave us a message, and we'll call you back!"

"Dad! It's Gina," I yelled into the phone. "Listen, you've got to get a camera crew down here at the camp. There's Big Foot running around here, and one of them got Frank! They say they're going to keep making trouble if—"

The machine beeped. It took only twenty-second messages, which is definitely a stupid idea. I mean, even when I have nothing to say I can talk for more than twenty seconds. And this time I had plenty to say. I drew in a long, shaky breath and dialed the number again. When the message was over, I continued.

"They're going to keep making trouble if we don't stop the construction of Mr. Creeley's new camp. He's building a whole bunch of new stuff, Dad, so we have to stop him, so you have to grab Ollie and get down here quick—"

The machine cut me off again.

I didn't dare call a third time. I was afraid of getting caught by Mr. Creeley. I just hoped I had gotten my point across in those two short messages. And I hoped he believed me! Ollie is short for Oliver, and he's my dad's camera operator.

They've gone to all kinds of dangerous places to-gether, doing news stories.

I was going over to the door to sneak out when I heard Stacey speaking in a nervous, high-pitched voice.

"Mr. Creeley!" she said, loudly, peeking over her shoulder to make sure I heard her. "Is the nurse in her office? It's time for me to take my asthma medication."

He said something to her, gruffly. There was no way I was going to make it out the door past him!

I dove behind his desk, then realized he was bound to go there if he walked into his office. I shimmied along the floor until I got to a file cab-inet and wedged myself behind it, facing the screened-in wall.

Just in time, too. Mr. Creeley told Stacey to go straight to the nurse's office, and never to walk around alone again. He banged the door shut as he walked into his office and sat down comfortably behind his desk.

I was trapped!

14

Escape!

I could hear Stacey moving around outside the office, wondering where the heck I was. Finally she came to the back and I tapped on the mosquito netting.

She gave a surprised little gasp when she saw me. I mean, I was standing right next to her—but on the other side of the mesh wall!

I put my finger over my lip. Mr. Creeley was dialing the phone. When the person on the other end picked up, he started yelling immediately.

"Jake! It's Hank. We can't start with the dynamite today!" He sounded really angry. "One of the campers is missing. I'm sure it's some kind of stunt, but we can't blast until we find him!"

Blast? *Dynamite*? No wonder the Big Foot were so desperate to get something done. They must have known the blasting was scheduled to start that day. Taking Frank hostage was the only way they could think of to stop it!

I went cold with fury. Just who did Mr. Creeley think he was, anyway? Leveling the woods with his machines and his dynamite. I thought of the raccoons, and the birds we had seen in the trees when we were fishing. How would Mr. Creeley like me to stick some dynamite in his living room while he was kicking back in his La-Z-Boy?

Meanwhile, Stacey was sawing at the mosquito netting with a little penknife that she carried in her pocket. "It's no use," she whispered.

"Yeah, I'll call you as soon as they find the brat," Mr. Creeley said into the phone. Then he hung up and started pacing around his office.

I was getting really nervous now. I was pretty well hidden when he was sitting down, but if he walked over to the other wall, he would see me!

Stacey saw exactly what I was afraid of, and she winked at me. Then she disappeared.

Just as I was beginning to think she had totally deserted me, I heard a high-pitched, screaming wheeze from the other side of the building. Mr. Creeley stopped pacing and listened. There was another wheeze, and he ran outside.

"Sorry—asthma attack—bad!" Stacey was saying when he reached her, well out of sight of the entrance to the office.

"I thought you were going to the nurse!" he barked, picking her up and carrying her toward the nurse's office. "Don't you know your parents could sue me for this?"

Oh, boy, this guy is all heart, I thought, rolling my eyes. But I didn't waste any more time. I raced out of the office as soon as I could. I was home free!

I knew exactly where I had to go next. The Big Foot were holding my brother hostage, so they probably went to their own safest place. Their cave, smack in the middle of the construction site. When I thought of how close Frank had been to getting blasted along with the rest of them down there, I wanted to scream! I had to get to him and make sure he was okay.

While I ran through the woods to the construction site, I thought of Stacey. I didn't know if I would have had the nerve to pull a stunt like that! If I could even have thought of it in the first place. I mean, she was totally brave! I had definitely underestimated her.

I had underestimated the run ahead of me, too. I hadn't realized how far the construction site was from the regular camp! It hadn't seemed that long when Oak was carrying me, but he was huge and traveled with enormous strides. I was just running along on my stubby, human-sized legs, and a run that took Oak twenty minutes was taking me more than an hour. But every time I wanted to stop and rest, I thought of Frank, alone with those giant bogeymen. I had a huge cramp in my side, but I couldn't stop moving, even when I thought that my legs would give way underneath me.

Finally, I caught a glimpse of those hulking yellow construction machines through the trees. They were crouched ominously around the clearing as I burst out of the woods.

The clearing had gotten a lot bigger since my last visit, and the ground was more torn up. There were spray-painted marks all over the rock wall. I guessed that was where the crew planned to start blasting.

This was no time for sightseeing, though. I searched along the wall for the entrance.

Darn it! I said to myself. I knew the entrance was near that funny-looking tree. And wasn't there a scraggly little bush near the opening? I ran frantically from bush to bush, looking for a cave, but I couldn't find anything. My heart was thudding, and I started checking each bush again, kicking at the earth.

"Oak!" I called out, pulling at bushes and pounding on the rocks with my fists. "Let me in. Frank, are you in there?"

It was starting to seem hopeless. I had run all this way, and now I couldn't find the entrance. Nothing looked quite the way it had the night I was there with Oak. For one thing, Oak had me slung over his shoulder, so all the scenery was upside down. But Mr. Creeley and his construction crew had already changed the layout of the clearing. They had destroyed all the landmarks.

Finally, after twenty minutes of scurrying back and forth, I had to sit down. I was crying, and my knuckles were raw and bleeding from pounding on the rocks. I was sunburned and filthy and miserable, and my brother was lost. I sank down, my back against the rock wall.

Suddenly, the ground seemed to open up. My heart leaped into my mouth as I tried to grab on to something. But it was no use. I was falling...and falling...and falling....

15

No Second Chances

Finally, I landed with a jolt.

At first, all I could see was stars.

I had landed really hard.

But after a few seconds my vision cleared, and my eyes grew accustomed to the dim light. Sure enough, I was surrounded by that same phosphorescent glow, and I could just make out some cave paintings.

I stood up shakily and squinted into the gloom. And then I saw them. Ten or twelve Big Foot, all standing there staring at me. And a small, pale figure, dwarfed by their size, looking scared and defenseless surrounded by them.

Frank.

I almost leaped out of my skin, I was so glad to see him.

He looked okay. A little shaken up, but basically okay. He gave a little wave and I waved back.

Now that I had found him, I wasn't sure what to do next. There I was, on the Big Foot home turf, alone with about a dozen huge creatures that could rip me to shreds. As I said before, they made Oak look puny, and he was bigger than my dad.

Now that I thought of it, where was Oak?

I didn't see him anywhere. I didn't have time to worry about him, though. I had to convince these goons to let my brother go!

"Okay, look," I said, trying to sound really sure of myself. "I know that you're really mad about the dynamite and stuff. But I think I've figured out a way to stop it, so you'd better give my brother back!"

The biggest Big Foot—I remembered that his name was Mica—gave a deep, throaty chuckle. "We'd *better?* Is that so?" Then he stopped laughing. "Listen to me, Human. We have given you all the chances you're getting. No more of your promises!"

He picked up Frank by the back of his jeans and lifted him effortlessly over his head.

Frank was just dangling there, helplessly. But he picked his head up, looked at me, and yelled, "Gina, run! I mean it. *Get out of here!*"

I didn't know what to do. There was no way I

was going to leave him here, with these monsters. But what the heck was I going to do? Stomp on their giant feet? Tickle them?

Suddenly I heard a voice behind me.

"Put him down," Oak said quietly.

Mica looked up angrily and waved Frank in Oak's direction. He said something forceful and furious, in a language I had never heard before. But the phrases were short and guttural, and I could just imagine what he was threatening to do.

"I said, *let him go*," Oak insisted. "We do not need him anymore. It is done."

Mica's whole expression changed. His face seemed to soften, and his hard, angry eyes dulled a little. They weren't glowing nearly as brightly as he eased Frank to the ground and let go of his belt. Then Mica and the others slunk back into the shadows.

I turned around to look at Oak. I wanted to ask him what he meant when he had said "It is done." But he was gone too.

Frank ran to me and grabbed my hand.

"Come on, what are you waiting for?" he wanted to know. We ran together toward a distant light, up through the mouth of the cave.

"What kind of stunt were you pulling back

there?" he hissed angrily at me as we ran along. "You could have gotten yourself killed, you dope!"

"Well, I wasn't going to leave you there," I snarled. I mean, a little gratitude was in order.

"Yeah, well, thanks," he said grudgingly as we finally made it out of the cave.

We were outside, the sun was streaming down, and my brother was safe and sound! I should have been ecstatic. But my stomach did a double flip as I heard Mr. Creeley shouting at us from the other end of the clearing.

"I knew it! There they are. Both of them!" He looked about ready to blow a gasket, he was so angry. He was red-faced and sweaty, and the little lock of hair he usually had neatly combed over the top of his head was hanging to the side in a tangled mess. His eyes were bulging.

Heidi and Tom were just behind him, and they looked totally relieved. I think Heidi had even been crying! Anyway, they ran to us and checked us over immediately.

"Man, am I glad to see you," Tom said to Frank, giving him a little shake and then hugging him.

"Are you okay? You sure? You're okay?" Heidi kept asking, over and over. She started crying again while I reassured her I was fine.

Boy, she sure was high-strung!

Mr. Creeley pushed past them and grabbed Frank and me by our T-shirts.

"All right, you little troublemakers," he said, threateningly.

"Mr. Creeley, I know you're angry, but they're *safe*," Heidi said, putting a hand on his arm. "Let's just get them back to their bunks so they can chill out, and we'll talk about it later."

"You think I care if they're all right?" Mr. Creeley snapped at her. She took a couple of steps back, shocked. "I should have gone ahead and blasted them to pieces while they were fooling around in that cave. They were just trying to stop me!"

"Hey, Mr. Creeley—" Tom started to say, but Creeley was on a roll.

"Listen to me, you kids. I don't know who sent you here—an environmental group, or what. But I'm going to take this whole area of forest apart as soon as I've got you stowed away down at the camp. And none of your orders of protection or documentation of endangered species is going to be able to stop me then!"

He shook us some more and laughed maniacally.

My head was rattling so much that I couldn't

speak, or I might have told him I had no idea what he was talking about!

"Hello, Mr. Creeley! Do you think you could see your way clear to putting down my kids?" A voice broke through the rattling. Frank and I were dropped abruptly. We looked up.

"*Dad!*"

He and Ollie had been standing in the trees the whole time, filming all of this!

"I've just found out some interesting information about you, Mr. Creeley," he said. "I've been hoping I could talk to you!"

"Well, I've got a few choice words for you," Mr. Creeley said. "Your kids are nothing but trouble. Just today, both of them disappeared and caused us a lot of worry!"

"Dad! *Dad!*" I said, tugging at his sleeve. "Talk to Mr. Creeley later. We've got to show you something!"

"What is it?" he asked, still looking at Mr. Creeley a little strangely.

"We have to show you the cave where the Big Foot live," Frank said, tugging on his other arm.

"Oh, now, kids—" Dad said, resisting, but Ollie was already fixing a little light at the top of his camera.

"Come on, Stan," he said. "Can't hurt. They might have found something interesting!"

"All right, all right," my dad muttered as he followed us into the cave.

I know it sounds kind of crazy to go back down into a cave full of angry beasts. But I really wanted my dad to see them. Then he could break the story, and Mr. Creeley would positively have to stop the construction. I knew the Big Foot would understand—if I could just explain before they took a bite out of us, that is.

As Frank and I led Dad and Ollie down into the cave, we told them about the Big Foot, how huge they were, and how cool the cave paintings were.

I didn't even notice that the glowing rocks seemed to be gone and that the ground was a lot rougher than it had been before. I wasn't paying attention at all until we rounded the last corner and both Frank and I realized at the same time...

The cave paintings were gone!

16

Spooky Scoop

We looked at each other, then back at the walls, where Ollie's halogen light was searching for any kind of picture at all.

"Is that one?" he asked, stopping at a rock.

"That's just a shadow," I told him. I was totally confused! Where had everything gone? Where were the Big Foot?

I ran through the route we had taken at lightning speed in my head.

There were no other passageways, no wrong turns we could have taken. The twists and turns were the same as they had been on the way out.

As Ollie shone his light around, I realized that this was the same cavern. It was the same shape, with the same stalactites and rock formations. But all evidence of the giant furry creatures was gone!

Creeley appeared behind us in the passageway, and he gave a start of surprise. I remembered that he had seen the paintings before—he had stolen that painted piece of rock to have it analyzed—and knew that he was just as shocked as I was.

"See?" he said, trying to cover himself. "There's nothing here at all. Obviously, these children are not to be trusted. You can take them home now."

"Creeley, these kids are geniuses," my dad said, turning around and facing him. "They made up that Big Foot story and staged Frank's disappearance because they knew it would get me up here. And they were right!" He turned to us and put his hands on our shoulders. "They obviously recognized that what you were doing was wrong, and they went out and broke the story to stop you. I'd trust them any day!"

"What are you talking about?" Mr. Creeley said. He started to walk out of the cave, but my dad was right behind him, and Ollie was filming everything.

"Mr. Creeley, you're building a new camp here, aren't you?" my dad asked.

"Well, yes, I am!" Mr. Creeley said, smiling sickeningly at the camera. "A whole new camp, with all the modern conveniences. There will be a pool, and air conditioning, and even a restaurant! Too bad you and your kids won't be able to join us there!"

"But, Mr. Creeley! Surely you're aware that this is a protected forest?" my dad continued as we reached the mouth of the cave. Mr. Creeley stopped, his grin frozen on his face.

"I looked into your records," my dad continued. "You've managed to get a blasting permit by showing fake maps to the government, sneaking it all past the Environmental Protection Agency!"

"Well, I—those maps—" Mr. Creeley was sputtering.

"I've got footage of you saying some pretty interesting things on camera already," my dad was saying, in his best I'm-a-reporter-who's-got-your-number voice. "What was that about an order of protection?"

"I—uh—well, that is...I was only speaking figuratively. Of course I wasn't planning to build anything here." He tried to smile, but he looked a little ill. "Oh! No, no!" Mr. Creeley assured Dad, waving his hands. Ollie panned his camera across the scene of the desolate clearing, the huge bulldozer, the crane, and the spray-painted marks.

"I'm *so* glad," my dad said, in that tone of

voice he uses when he catches me watching Letterman when I'm supposed to be asleep.

"No, I recently changed my plans," Mr. Creeley finally said. "There isn't going to be any construction."

17

Worms and Eyeballs

"Blindfold the initiate," a voice intoned.

There was no way I could mistake that voice—it was definitely Linda behind that mask.

I felt a musty bandanna being pulled over my head and tied at the back so I couldn't see. My knees were sore from kneeling on the ground behind the cabin, and I felt like a total idiot.

But I had to admit, it was kind of fun.

I felt hands pulling me up on my feet, and I stepped forward hesitantly.

"Don't worry," I heard Stacey whisper. "We won't let you bump into anything."

I walked a little more confidently, letting their hands guide me along. I knew the cabin well enough to be able to tell I was going in the back door. But something brushed against my face as I went through the doorway—it felt like pieces of string.

"Watch out for the cobwebs!" Rebecca said, giggling. "I hope those black widow spiders aren't still there!"

"Shhh!" someone else hissed. We went inside the cabin and stopped.

"Put out your hands, and feel the dead worms," Linda commanded.

I stuck out my hand, and someone pushed it into a bowl filled with something disgusting and squishy. Wet, cold spaghetti!

"Eeew!" I couldn't help saying.

"Silence!" Linda barked. I heard more giggling, and I tried to keep my own mouth from cracking into a smile.

"Now you must eat the eyeballs! These are the eyeballs of last year's new campers who didn't make it through the initiation. Open your mouth!"

I opened my mouth dutifully and felt something cold, round, and wet. I didn't know what it was, and I wanted to spit it out. I knew it wasn't anything really bad, but they *had* just said "eyeballs," and the whole idea grossed me out.

Then I recognized the taste. Olives!

I hate olives, but they're not eyeballs. I grinned, then chewed it up and swallowed.

"Yum," I murmured.

"Do you swear to uphold the honor and secrets of Camp Slumbering Pines?" Linda demanded to know.

"What secrets?" I asked.

"Silence, initiate! You have to swear!" She pinched me on the arm.

"Ow! Okay, I swear," I said, dissolving into giggles completely. Everybody cheered, and the blindfold came off. The next thing I knew, I was being bombarded with Silly String.

"Hey!" I held up my arms, trying to fend off the attack, but I was totally covered in pink goo within seconds.

Boy, if my friends from home could see me, they'd think this was pretty stupid, but I was actually having fun. I was glad I had decided to stay.

The day before, when my dad wrapped up his news segment, he had taken me and Frank aside and thanked us for the great story. "These environmental stories are really hot right now," he told us. "The network is going to love this. You kids should be really proud. You helped preserve the forest, and you got people's attention to do it."

We did feel pretty proud.

Frank even elbowed me in the ribs and grinned at me!

I was so amazed, I almost missed the next thing my dad said.

"If you guys want to come home for the rest of the summer, I'd love to have you," he was saying. "Your mom agrees. You've proven that you know how to handle yourselves. You can stay home without a sitter."

We stared at each other, dumbfounded.

I mean, a week before, I would have busted out of that camp so fast it would make your head spin.

But then I thought about the raccoon family in the woods by our bunk. And the birds and trees Heidi was telling us about. I also thought about Stacey, and how she had stood up to Mr. Creeley just for me. And Linda's major crush on Frank! I had to see what was going to happen there.

"We want to stay," Frank and I had said at the same time. Dad just shook his head and laughed.

"Two city mice, out here in the country," he said, looking around at the scenery. "I sure envy you two!" He gave both of us hugs, and kisses from Mom, then got into his Jeep and drove away.

And now here I was, curled up in a sleeping bag with Silly String in my hair, whispering and gossiping with the rest of the bunk after lights-out.

Everyone was pretty wiped out. The other girls dropped off to sleep pretty quickly, but I just lay there, looking out the screen wall of my cabin into the deep, dark night.

It's funny—I was so scared of that darkness and those woods when I first came to Camp Slumbering Pines. I didn't know what was out there, and even the trees seemed like a threat.

But now that I had spent some time here, the darkness was kind of comforting. In the city, with the streetlights and everything, it never really gets dark. Out here, though, you can close and open your eyes, and you can hardly tell the difference.

I started thinking about everything that had happened that day. It was great that we had managed to help the Big Foot, but I wasn't sure how it had happened.

I mean, there we were, in the cave with the paintings—except there weren't any paintings! We called my dad to do the story on the Big Foot, but they disappeared when he showed up.

It was as if they knew he'd do the story anyway—on the protected forest.

Where had they gone?

My mind was racing, but I was totally exhausted. I was about ready to fall asleep myself when I caught those red, gleaming eyes looking at me.

"Oak!" I whispered, wide awake again.

I got up quietly and slipped out the door. He had already replaced the concrete slab that he'd tossed into the woods a few nights ago, and I sat down on it.

He sat near me, a little farther from the cabin.

"I brought my dad into the cave, but you and the other Big Foot were gone," I said. "Where did you go?"

"We were there," Oak answered. "But not there. We did not want to meet your father."

"Well, it was pretty embarrassing, you know," I told him. "I mean, there I was telling him about these giant creatures, and now he probably thinks I'm a total doofus."

"Not a doofus," Oak corrected me. "Just a girl with an active imagination."

"Oh, great," I moaned. "Thanks a lot."

"You didn't need us anymore," he went on. "It was done."

"That's what you said before. What does it mean? What was done?"

"Your father was aware of the forest problem. He was doing what was necessary to stop the construction. And so the barrier between our world and yours was restored. Things are now as they should be. No Humans may enter the Shadow Zone—unless we allow them to."

"Wait! Is that why we couldn't see the paintings when my dad was there? You wouldn't let us into the Shadow Zone?"

"Correct." Oak nodded. "You Humans can see the paintings only when you're in the Shadow Zone. When we didn't need you anymore, we closed the Zone to you."

"Yeah, well, I guess my dad would have freaked out when he saw you, anyway. But I still the think the Zone would have been a lot better off with someone like Linda, or even Heidi. At least they know more about running around in the woods and stuff."

Oak grinned, and he didn't look nearly as scary now that I knew him a little better. But I couldn't help sneaking a peek at his huge, nasty, threatening teeth one more time.

"Man, I thought you were going to tear me apart and have me for breakfast with those things," I said. Oak made a really weird, whiny noise. I was totally freaked until I realized he was laughing.

"What is so funny?" I demanded.

"Tear you apart!" He gave his little whinny

again. "Gina, look at my teeth. Carefully."

I inspected them, but I still didn't get it.

"Look carefully. Wide, flat molars, Gina! Like a horse's."

Like a—

"But horses eat grass!" I yelped.

"No ripping. No tearing! All we can do with these things is grind. We don't even eat meat— never mind Humans." Oak really thought this was a great joke.

I groaned and hit my forehead with my hand. "I knew I should have watched that *National Geographic* special more carefully."

I looked back at Oak, who was still laughing. Actually, he was kind of cool-looking, in a heavy metal kind of way.

Not that I wanted to hang out with him or anything.

"Don't worry," he said, as if he knew what I was thinking. "Now that everything is okay, you Humans won't bother us, and we won't bother you—or anyone. Maybe the occasional howl to keep the tourists coming back. That should make Mr. Creeley happy."

"Oh, he's leaving the camp," I told him. "His sister is taking over after all. I guess if he couldn't make a million bucks, he didn't want to go to the trouble of running the camp!"

Oak nodded. "Then you won't be seeing us again at all. Or hearing us."

"Well—I hope everything is cool with you guys. Thanks for the...um...hospitality. And the history lesson!"

"And thanks for all your help," Oak answered.

He was walking into the woods, between two trees, when the night air was split by a long, desolate howl.

"Hey, I thought we weren't going to hear you guys anymore," I said, laughing.

Oak looked up, sniffing the air curiously.

Then he shrugged. "I don't know who that was. It sounded like a Big Foot, but it wasn't anyone from my clan...."

With that he disappeared into the woods completely.

Suddenly I realized what he had just said.

"Your *clan*? Wait! Do you mean there are other families out there? Oak! *Oak!*"

But the only thing that answered me was another howl, somewhere deep in the woods of the Cascade Mountains....

**Don't miss the next book in the
Shadow Zone series:
MY TEACHER ATE MY HOMEWORK**

I stared at my knapsack. The doll was in there with my books, and I had to get rid of it.

What if I really *had* created a voodoo doll of my teacher? Then whatever I did to the doll would happen to Mrs. Fink. If I tossed it in the bay, would Mrs. Fink end up drowning in her bathtub?

Suddenly, the buckle to my knapsack began to move. *All by itself.* While I sat, frozen, one side unbuckled. Then the other.

The flap opened. A small arm poked out. I gasped as the head of the doll swiveled toward me and blinked its glassy gray eyes.

"Hello, Jesse," the doll said. "We meet at last."